BEAUTIFUL
SOON ENOUGH

BEAUTIFUL
SOON ENOUGH

MARGO BERDESHEVSKY

FC2

TUSCALOOSA

The University of Alabama Press
Tuscaloosa, Alabama 35487-0380

Copyright 2009 by Margo Berdeshevsky
All rights reserved
First Edition

Published by FC2, an imprint of the University of Alabama Press, with support
provided by Florida State University, the Publications Unit of the Department of
English at Illinois State University, and the School of Arts and Sciences, University
of Houston–Victoria

Address all editorial inquiries to: Fiction Collective Two, University of Houston–
Victoria, School of Arts and Sciences, Victoria, TX 77901-5731

⊗

The paper on which this book is printed meets the minimum requirements of
American National Standard for Information Sciences—Permanence of Paper for
Printed Library Materials, ANSI Z39.48–1984

Library of Congress Cataloging-in-Publication Data
Berdeshevsky, Margo.
  Beautiful soon enough / Margo Berdeshevsky. — 1st ed.
      p. cm.
  Includes bibliographical references.
  ISBN-13: 978-1-57366-149-2 (pbk. : alk. paper)
  ISBN-10: 1-57366-149-X (pbk. : alk. paper)
  1. Women—Fiction. I. Title.
  PS3602.E7514B43 2009
  813'.6—dc22

                              2009017212

Book Design: Theresa O'Donnell and Tara Reeser
Cover Design: Lou Robinson
Typeface: Baskerville
Produced and printed in the United States of America

Moi, je mords la terre comme un fruit

—Jeanne Moreau

So she left,
to remember
fictions of a
passion
to burst my hearts,
darkness
to green a garden—
a fact of myth,
of woman

Contents

WINDOW

She hated Saint Valentine's Day. A woman in a garter belt.

And a moth who feeds on spice.

The woman stands in the beige lace belt, which is a gift that was in her mailbox this morning. She had said —I will not celebrate love's day anymore, unless or until some good man leaves me beautiful lingerie in my letter box.

And then it happened. She is standing at her window, wearing the gift.

Outside, it is Wednesday noon, and beautifully, delicately, snowing. Inside, she is warm and she is at her window. Below in the flying snow, he is watching. She makes a sign with the fingers of one hand, like a butterfly, and he knows he may visit, now.

When he enters her room, it is with another small gift, a square thing wrapped three times, in tissue papers the color of chrysanthemums. The mauve, the plum, the deepest red. She opens it like an eager child. A tiny cricket cage, like the ones in street markets in Hong Kong. Not a cricket in it, though; a spice moth.

A woman in a garter belt. A man who understood her need.

She takes the wonderful new gift and carries it to the window and she opens it quickly; sends the moth out into the fluttering white. —It will die, he says.

She frees the man, as she closes the blind.

He will forever speak of this woman.

No wife can bear to listen.

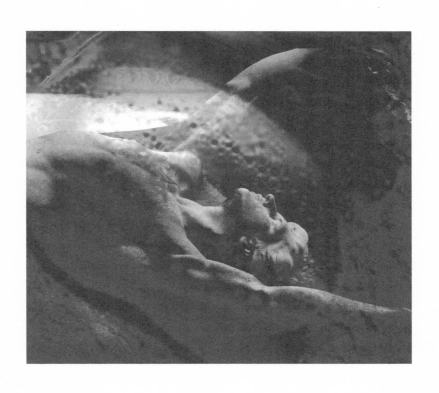

CANNIBAL NOTES

There will be no action in the street for hours.

Dawn before hot rolls or crows, before monks and nuns in woolen hoods and naked feet, and kneeling. She has an hour in the church-candle darkness before the crazed neighbor she's fascinated by comes in with his cologne again, louder than incense, seducing her. He's manic and she can seduce him back, pew to pew, prayer to prayer—windows filling with Christ and him rocking on the balls of his feet when he prays. He says she has Magdalene eyes. Do monks love like this? She doesn't know.

But in her early hour she's quiet in her tight black coat, and there's no eau de toilette yet. She's heard madmen wear a lot of scent on purpose but that they can't help it. There's a dark place, like a womb, where she's waiting for the holy to rock her senseless. To split the top of her head with her soul thrusting her; she'd like a lick of it please: obsession is awake again.

And the man who is on heavy doses, who doesn't want to take what he's been given to calm what rages in him, who doesn't want to take it or be crazy either, wants help, and he's praying for it. Wants a sign. He's heard that mania's a spiritual crisis, hasn't he? Curling like a baby, all two meters of him. He thinks she has holy answers, which she does; she's worked on answers. She's praying to let her help him, heal him.

It doesn't work.

But now, his choir-boy eyes and baritone have her attention. And with her eyes closed, serenity is distracting her heart. And she thinks maybe love would be enough.

The man comes an hour late, sleeps in, arrives later than she— the neighbor lady who's getting too psychically connected to his story which is dire as a church fire. In her flat, alone, she wakens with his nightmares, in the darkest before dark. She heads for the church pews, long before pigeons are ruffling in their gutters. Before the monks. Driven by nightmare and perfume and piety. He'll be there in a little while, she knows.

An hour, and then a singing mass, to pray harder with the other rats and frogs in the baptismal fonts, that's what they call them: church-rats, moles. Morning after morning, penitence, until they get an Alleluia. A lady with healing hands, everybody says, healing hands, but it's femininity roused by her neighbor's perfume. Does anybody else notice the waft at the side door when he strides in from the chill, old pipe smoke in his pocket and clinging to his clothes?

A morning breed apart, before dawn. Before clanging, lauding bells, and the sun.

The monastic order files in: white, woolen, boys left, girls right, fervent as a tide drowning everything that isn't sacred.

But she has a purpose. She'd like to have a turquoise-light epiphany, to drown in dark heaven, in this Romanesque church around the corner from where they both live, at number 22, second floor front, hers, fifth floor rear, his. Both hurrying here, some sixty gargoyles, saints, and a revolution of dragons in her hair. Who's the manic here and how does she know it's him?

He confesses every morning to her after the last bells when they go to have café au lait, after they've had the wafer and the blood of wine. Now the sun is sneaking up, and the good monks tucked back in their ordinary robes with no hoods—do they have hormones? He confesses. He wants to love women. All women.

She with a wafer of wisdom over the perfume, and the man, the man, the man—he's dead certain that her optimism and hands can save his life before the crows. Of course she wants to, she desperately wants to, or they would not both be there at this deep-cut well.

She wishes a storm would come.

They don't want depression; they do want rolls and marmalade; don't want chaos; they like Gregorian chants; they want a sign. She wants a sign. Not a nest of dead birds.

If one of the living infants falls from a nest and is touched—its mother, were she singing still, would not let it back in. After the fall, if there is a fall, who truly loves a survivor? Not the nest. It falls through the damp air to embrace the ground, tongue-kissed only once, and now a cannibal for God, or love, or which?

Again, she takes him home. It doesn't work. He says again that she looks to him like Magdalene.

Takes him home and lets him try, and he stops dead in the middle and says he is going to become a eunuch. He says theirs is not a love story and he is too sad and too French, so she concentrates on healing him, on his shoes, on Jesus; she tries, asks for secret spells, listens to his sorrow; she suggests love, he threatens he'll drown in the river. She suggests exercise and a change of scenery: a camel ride in a desert, an island. Instead, he gets married. Rather soon, she thinks. To a lady far away.

He sends her a postcard to praise her. She doesn't go to morning mass very often, anymore.

The monks and frogs and rats don't notice.

She goes once. Once—more. Dawn before hot rolls or crows. On the way out of church, at that same side door, there is a blind man on the steps. He pulls her arm as if he knows her. Wants to whisper to her and only her. —*I'll give you two-thousand euros if you can make me see the sunrise.* They are standing on winter-silver steps, light of all colors coming on. She spends this one cold hour trying with every word she knows until all the sun is up and cloud-dead, and she has not convinced the blind man of anything other than that he is blind and she can talk.

There will be no sunset.

—I'm sorry.

She's broken, and useless for truth or humanity, neither of which the blind man paid for; things that take an hour cost more. Always, she knows, in winter when the light goes, her stride turns black, however holy. And she picks up strangers for their heat. An hour is not very long to undo. She's hungry as a crow.

A Friday Desdemona

Othello is holding a dime-store mirror up over their heads, so she can see herself as he plunges. —Look, dear. *Sweeting.* Look.

It is full-length. He holds it up with one arm, the other under and around her white body.

He'd like to touch the skin in the mirror.

He has a virgin again. He will play the Moor far better tonight.

The darkness turns inside out, flame-sideways-upside. This is heart medicine. My love, are we dying?

—Would you like to wear this? He holds a white woven robe, fit for a death scene.

I'm not a star-fucker. I'm a girl who makes him pay attention. I'm white and large-thighed. I'm new passion. I'm cougar-eyed just like him. I'm desperate for peace. I'm a lover, not a warrior. I'm courageous. I'm rain. I'm a liberal. I'm not my mother.

—Look at yourself, *Sweeting*.

Later he says —Would you be my Friday date? Every Friday, come here. He strokes her like a rabbit.
But she wants more.
Later he says —Don't ask for the impossible. Later he says —Hit me if you want to.

The stairs smell of cat piss. Homeless piss. He's on the third floor. The door is the color of rust. It has a heavy iron bolt, which he opens.

Uptown is my mother. I think she wants him. It enrages me. But I believe in peace.
I keep *The Times*' theatre section, with his pictures. She's always looking at them.

Downtown, there's a man crouching against a car, leaning with his cardboard sign that says: I am hungry. I am hungry. I am hungry. Until he runs out of space. I want to save him. And I'm afraid of him.

Further downtown, up the fetid stairs and behind the bolted door, Othello lays me down. I'm his sheet; for his brown marble skin. I'm spilled white.

And if I love thee not, chaos is come again.
Until we run out of time.
He has to go.

Now he doesn't need a mirror. Now he can teach her.
But the silly girl wants love.
He's playing a warrior. A killing machine. Othello. A soldier. He
keeps that in mind. He can never stop thinking. But he can't stop
thinking about her, either. Her fire, her rain, her pale peach lace. He
is jealous of that. Only that.

The distinction between war and loss will be blurred to the van-
ishing point. She wants to hold him back. His will to kill. His murder
of what is not her. There are no definable battlefields or fronts. Just
a large bed behind a bolted door and his collected Shakespeare, his
scripts stacked up for a headboard. And her. A child who holds the
warrior's huge hand by the fingertips. This man has a shield and she
wants to break it. Pierce it. He closes his eyes.

A pungent Lower East Side fume, where she walks back out into
the furnace of a July afternoon, attacks. She sees herself in every
window, a girl who's just been had by a great man. She whispers —*I
cannot understand the darkness of you.* But a street can't answer.

She tries on Saint Joan's armor. A dress. A Friday date. It does
not fit. She's only a student. *Light your fire, do you think I dread it as much
as the life of a rat in a hole? You promised me my life but you lied!*

—Why won't you let it work? I'm your lover. I'm not a warrior.
I'm real. She's shouting.

—Hit me if you want to. He says it again.

When he first saw her, she was white flesh and too young, but he
loved what he saw. The ghost-eyed courage. She was playing Saint
Joan. *Light your fire*, her legs planted, sixteen summers urgent, theatre
pounding down between her thighs.

A great actor plays his Othello again and again, in different seasons of his life. He waited. An artist can wait for his inspirations. Everything in its time.

And then, a few weeks of coupling, and that was enough. He would remember her when he needed to, when the actress in his arms was too pale. When he was alone, and she had no name. That, he liked.

He's an enormous man in the director's row; he holds me pinioned with an ice-cougar gaze like claws on my nipples. He wants to touch where I am not revealed.

He waits until I am of age. Then we lie as though it were a fact. No mention of love allowed, in his bowery room, three flights up from the bridge, to hold his shoulders which are museum marble. Which are smooth. To hold his beard as if I could tear it out.

—You are war. A man who does not even sweat. He holds a mirror up over our parallel bodies like Atlas holding the globe with one arm.

A Friday date.

Inevitably, she loves. Inevitably, he won't. Peace and war and loss.

—Honey, don't count on me. Don't wait for a promise. It won't come.

War. I'm Desdemona in a shroud. I cling to the black marble of the actor's arms. The Moor's arms. How quiet the quiet is, in a city of loss. I have a useless heart. I'm ready for just about anything. Sex. Hostility. God. He is a killing machine. He refuses to lie.

New York City devours me like the last frontier buffalo's entrails. I shout more as I march until blisters swell and burst and ooze into my boot leather. I'm hating how we had a very quiet war and never loved. I kept a calendar of how many times he had me. Put my skin in his earth. In his teeth. Finer than Olivier, more surprising than Welles. Love's *deus ex machina*, and vengeance, its inexorable script. Scripts

askew behind the mattress, stacked with all his reviews, stapled. Pills
for being too human. Raves for being the Classics' modern mister.
I'm your solitary fantasy, right here in your bed. Look at me! Curtain
up and curtain down. I loved how you killed me, with your socks still
on. It all only lasted what? A couple of weeks. A pebble in a machine,
a war that kept on killing. Its wheel, huge.

I always thought it was my mother. How she flounced, when he
called. I thought she read my calendar, my tiny white diaries on hot
summer mornings in my closed blue-papered bedroom, and that she
called him up and said —You stay away. Understand, Othello, our
girl has a future. My armchair-liberal mother wanted a safe white
daughter, that summer when dark James Chaney was strung from his
Mississippi oak.

Under a canopy of gauze, *you* bring out the hip-grinding jazz.
The Robeson recordings, a singing riverine bass note, even deeper
than yours. Bring out a caftan for a queen. Blackberry wine, after the
mirror, and before you send me back to my mother. My mother's copy
of "John Brown's Body" high on her bookshelf, her prized portrait of
a drumming African, crooked on our foyer wall. —Like that?
    There's a candlelight march all through those summer nights. I
wheel around and around the courthouse, that July, my black man
who is not mine, who is the warrior of ancient Venice and is not mine,
is not there. He does not defend. He does not raise his sword or word.
He does not argue, does not fight for me with Black Power fists. He
listens to my mother's warning and puts out the light. Just like that.
    I'm a white rain; lost, paraffin sizzling my fingernails, melting
the night.
    He says —Hit me if you want to. And he goes to sleep.
    Like that.
    I'm not a warrior. I'm tired. I'm a buffalo. I'm the sacrifice. No,
of course that's not it. I light a new candle under my dead mother's

photograph. The paper catches fire and I have to douse it. In the crimson light I'm stabbing at forgiving her, like a slimed fish, but its eyes are open.

I read his book.

In the window next to an ice cream store and passing by a vat of the fudge marble-brickle, I see his famous face. *You*, on a publisher's cover. Brightened. Blurred. If I get in touch what will he do? He'll send me a daisy. A caftan. I pass ten broken telephones. He'll go... *Sweeting*, see how beautiful you are? Thank you for wearing silk. And thank you for removing it. A hunter's orange grin. A warrior's red basso. My mother definitely wanted him.

There's one reunion, in his bed, after my divorce. I whisper —Help? Please? Couldn't you help me to shine, too?

—You know we're family, honey. The first is always family, he says, cello-voiced. Renowned. The best Othello since...

A collection of bottled and capped sentinels lines up on his kitchen counter in a wooded upstate canyon. He is huge. More huge than before. He pops something yellow and small and dizzying under my nose in the sweet darkness, and surrounds me. More giant than before.

The darkness turns inside out, drugged shadows, burning flame sideways-upside, once again. But this is heart medicine. Are we dying?

—Would you like to wear this? He holds a white woven robe fit for a death scene. —Can you only love a Desdemona? I finally punch at the black marble that can't break. Nothing in him breaks. A star. Who does not mind guns. I punch. He doesn't shatter at all. My tight white knuckles hit. Go on, hit. Hate. Be a warrior, woman. Lovers do not last.

The girl makes him feel too old. He sends her off with a white caftan tucked into her purse for a present. The best he can give.

I have no eyes. I have no body. It is the quality of having power to be loved. It is something men need from women and that they do not get. It is the cause, Othello: So put out the lights.

I'm wearing peach lace pants. At the fountain near the Plaza Hotel. I like how the air slips up and under my loose high-polished legs. Men notice my leather skirt. With snaps. From Rome. It flaps as I walk. My knees show, silken. I speed-walk to hard and crazy tubas. Loud. I zoom like a blowfly. I dig deep in my pocket for a snippet of string to tie it around a rusted rod of a tall iron fence to proclaim that I was here. Because of that slide, there, I skinned my knee and needed iodine. See? I lived at number eight with the red canopy. Right over there. My mother wanted my black Othello. My skinned right knee hurts. I am a grey stone, in the middle of Fifth Avenue, all the telephones are broken.

I knock on your new uptown door. I'm a detective. I found you. And you peer out at me through venetian blinds, holding a hammer.

—Nothing, I say. Just hello. And I hold our gaze through the slats. You remember too, but not exactly my name. I have no name for you. Damn. I can tell.

—I was just walking, and I needed you.

—Of course you did. Basso fame, old Shakespearean chuckling. Unlatching the chain, grudgingly. An old man's gamble.

You really cannot think what to call me.

—Do you want to come in?

—I'm ok, Luke. You're startled by the use of your first name; no one ever uses it. Hey, cougar. I'm prowling. I'm out checking my fence posts. I extend my hand. Press his flesh.

A sound like an old warship moving metal through ice. You're going to like me, soldier.

But I turn on one runner's toe and bound away, Olympian, through the open window. A blowfly. A gadfly.

Brava. This was courage.

You don't applaud or call after me. But I feel your innuendo lifting my hair. I turn back and wave once, without commitment, like a baby to a rich relation.

I begin counting men with puma eyes. Wars.

I want to sign my name on black marble like a veteran.

I declare war on peace and happiness. Its chronic blur. On peace.

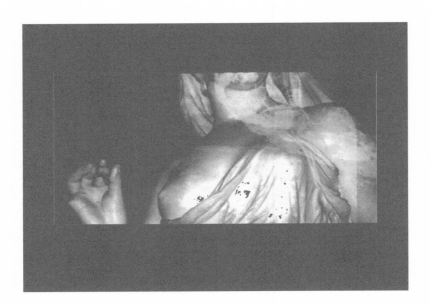

RETRO

There are no bombs here, but the continued threats. Only in other cities now. And just outside, blossom after blossom flames, pretty as a Japanese print: spring.

He comes to her bed wearing a single long white opera glove. It's meant to titillate, and it does. Surprise her. And it does. This is the hand that can wipe away dead skin. And dead sex. And dead love. She knows this. Why else would she bed a married man?

The glove has been snatched from his coat pocket en route to the room. As soon as she sees it, it will kill her or kindle her. And she has to decide.

Kill me, she tells him. Kill the woman who cannot love anymore. Kill the woman who tells lies about lives and burrows in city caves, hungry. Kill me, darling man, and then, turn me on again.

The glove is shining in the curtained noon-light. The man is a *cinq-à-sept* lover who visits at twelve because she lets him. The so-French notion of the lover who is available at a specified hour, five to seven, one to three, has a distinct taste, like a *foie gras*, like balsamic.

The glove or the raised skin, which to kiss? The glove or the ghost of dead ones and darling ones? She kisses the satin fingertips, lets them dawdle, lets them trace, lets them enter. Lets them circle her heavy breasts and lighter breath. Lets them and invites them. Growls and then sings to them, a song her father taught her, a Russian lullaby: *Byyyyyooshki—byyyyooo. Byyyy-ooo-shki—byyyyoooo.*

The man with the glove has opened his eyes, and is he crying? Cry, darling. Touch me with satin, let me sing my father's lullaby to you and let me see you cry.

The hand, his shining, sequined, satin hand, is doing what it must. And she won't stop the singing. Won't let him stop crying. She knows how to do a little theatre too, sweet-thing. He's done what was expected, surprised her. Suggested. Stroked. Stopped. Now she wants the glove. Now the dance. Now the dark. Now the ghosts. Now the game.

But before she puts it on, she will wipe his tears with it. Consider murder, a shining white tying; decide again, she's a better woman than such a story. Go home, darling. Now, you've surprised me, toddle on home, sweet-thing. Kiss me once more, and I won't expect a thing.

He leaves without his glove. Dresses wordlessly in her hallway. Does not tell her when or if he will return. She doesn't expect him to. Remains damply, easily amid her pillows. When the door click happens—when the sound of steps descending—when the wind at the window makes its rustle among the newly budding geraniums—when the shadow on the wall opposite the goldenrod tree, affirms that this is springtime and sacred with new things: she opens the package from a woman far away.

A gift of spring? A new weapon? She never knows what Martine will send her. It always has a perfume of French lavender wafting from the package. This time it comes from a city she's never seen. She wouldn't open the package this morning. Told herself no, after the lover leaves. I'll wait until he leaves, and then I'll open it.

Now she slits the scotch-tape with her sharpest fingernail. Opens the folds as delicately as in any lovemaking. Finds the penciled note that says, "Remember, ma chère, a woman needs to improve her technique, no matter how old she gets. Remember, ma chère. With love as ever, Martine."

She has opened the tissue paper, which again, and as usual, is scented lavender. And she extracts a pair of leopard's paws, smooth, silken, ready to be worn.

Wearing the leopard skin gloves, now, she dresses for the afternoon. For the springtime. For the mirror.

There's a noise she is not waiting for. Scratching like—a light knocking—and again a scratching, as of unsheathed nails on her door.

Her heart has sped to a tremble. Shivered more like winter, won't stop thrumming, insists she answer.

The leaves outside are gold, giving way to scuffed purple in the dark.

Naked-handed, naked-armed, ready for the real thing, this time, the married man has returned for the woman who is wearing feral gloves to wipe away the dead skin, and the dead sex, and the dead love. Why else bed a woman who could ruin him?

The carved wooden bed attacks them until there is no more sunlight, no more gloves, no more tears.

If I had no hands, then I might love you more kindly, each said, with no voice, and their eyes averted.

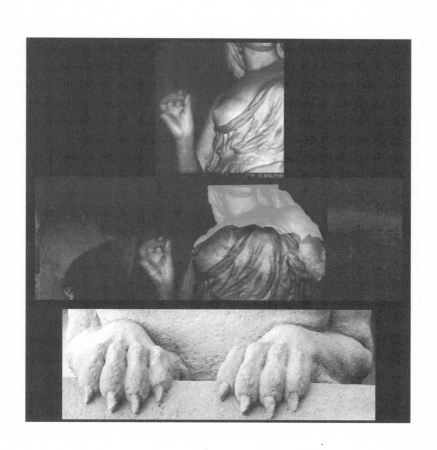

"Goodness had nothing to do with it."

—*Mae West*

BEFORE THE SECOND TASTE

She returns to the city where she was born, like a woman with a fear of spiders. Rich men harbor here. No one will blame her for hunting. Pull in, pull in like a tall ship. She does not have to go to the childhood playground, or the lobby where they carried out her corpses.

Her mother, drunk in heaven, puts on face cream, suggests she do the same. If the other women are thinner and your black clothes are inelegant, have lovely skin. Fingertips have eyes. When you are touched, you will be remembered.

Maybe she'll stop into the kinder lobbies, say a shy hello to a grown-old doorman, blacker, more arthritic. He's not the one who taught her how to ride a bicycle, up and down the rose granite sidewalks of East Ninety-Second Street. Don't tell this doorman that you used to live on the fourteenth floor here, 14B, facing silhouetted water towers.

Water towers looked like the top hat Toulouse-Lautrec wore when he hobbled and hunched after young and beautiful bodies. When she was little, her mother had wanted to see the José Ferrer movie, and dragged her along. She hid her eyes as the dwarf-legged black-hat cripple grinned at his women, Always, after, sky-ghost silhouettes beyond her bedroom window reminded her, frightened her, before she slept.

She thinks instead of the boy who rubbed against her body in the hall outside the family apartment. One of the boys. She did it after every date. Thinks of his hardened secret against her skirt, a coat, eased open. Of how she pushed and pushed delicately, almost pretending nothing was happening. Brushing in the in-place pulse, until everything was happening, and he lifted her up and down and up and down against his cloth, against him, against his belt, his hands pulling her tighter and trembling for the standing and the rocking balance, cloth-groin with cloth-groin. The jazzed drums of the position hard to the wall where her mother's collected Mexican tin and golden glass-eyed masks looked on, mute and without judgment. Lifted, and slid, a ballerina lift, a boy stammering against her adolescent and buttoned eagerness to climb him, and to extend, and to dazzle. Until she sent him home.

Again and again, she lets the wooden-paneled and gated cage bring them both up, the older man's hand on his polished lever, eyes on the polish. The younger boy at her side, impatient in the elevator mirror, where she eyed her beauty, for what was about to follow. How a boy's one hidden finger informed her inner palm, the blatant code. And then and then and then, pleased, exploded, young. Him, good-night, in the elevator re-called. She listened to its metal-rope music, oiled cables, their gilded cage turned in descent, before she turned her door key. And every cell of hers, a pleased vibrato, released. And him, a boy stopped just before it was too late. Young boys, Lautrec-crippled.

She returns to the city where she was born. She wants to toss her hairdo in some caged mirror. Or find a wealthy dinner companion, worthy of her. Stand in the cold evening on Ninety-Second Street.

And all the waiters have retired.

•

The seduction is the taste of frogs' legs and calves' brains simmered in crushed garlic. Clarified butter, a teaspoon of luncheon wine, miniscule chips of chive and curly parsley sprigs. Not a complicated recipe. A taste that stains the day like perfume on light raw silk.

•

They've shaved their legs and it is the first time. The skin underneath their arms, a little reddened. Each is sitting on a corner of the taller girl's turquoise bedspread, stroking her own smooth shins and knees, ignoring the other burning. This is being women. So is the golden square packet to hold a monthly number of tampons each gives the other as a gift. They have been suspended for one week from Nightingale Bamford School for young females, for smoking long and thin Salem cigarettes in the second floor bathroom, and laughing boldly back at the teacher who discovered them. They are caught with the mint and silver-colored pack in their can't-stop-laughing grasp. Unrepentant, they have bought each other the square, golden, imitation-leather pouches, matching initialed cigarette cases. They have the same initials.

—Don't be jealous. They're sharing a cover. I met him at the ballet in the balcony and I never told you. He's old.

There is quiet. Then they light one another's cigarettes in the dark.

—I have a favor with consequences, the taller adolescent who wears a C–cup and high-heeled mules announces. They're sharing the peach-scented cream for aftershave. Her voice stutters with nerves and she coils her arms around herself hiding nothing, as she launches.

The beginning of the favor is the planned luncheon to be cooked by her Vincent who is trim-bearded and thirty, and who she loves. She is adored.

The rounder girl checks her beauty in the elevator mirror floating up to apartment 16A, over Seventy-Second Street and the East River, where the mother is at nine-to-five work, the Barrymore-ish father has left for Hollywood and is not succeeding, is drinking, and his daughter is in a man's thrall. A father able to kill.

Vincent opens the tall girl's door, *The Magic Flute* pours out with the aroma of heating garlic, butter, frogs' legs, and brains. His gaze is nearly as turquoise as the spread the girls shaved upon. This man has probably lain there too. The round girl offers her most sophisticated handshake.

—You have peacock-colored eyes, she announces, for greeting. He kisses her on both cheeks, mindful of his beard.

—Are you French?

They are still in the doorframe. Her best friend who has the same initials as she does stands just behind him, is nearly as tall as he is, excited and more nervous and so becomes more languid, to cover it. She is pretending to hum the Mozart. The round girl eases into the familiar living room which is unfamiliar now, a room of aromas.

And the man is charmed with his young sweetheart's plan.

The white china platter arrives wafting garlic steam. The guest bites delicately, her first taste of legs and brains. I've heard that it is supposed to taste like chicken, and I've heard that cannibals, well, I mean someone said human flesh tastes like chicken too. The man nods passively, appreciatively, adult. The creases at his eyes are now a feature in the girl's gathering of details. Age.

He allows a beige cashmere arm to gather his girl nearer with illegal and protective affection. —And you have the same initials and your birthdays are two days apart in November, am I right? I find that very lovely. But other than that, you are each entirely your own persons, a rare thing at any age. The girls giggle just long enough to embody the age they both are. Thirteen-and-a-half.

The one under his light embrace presents her plan. The continuation of the favor she asks. Her actor-father is remaining in Hollywood and is determined that she come to live with him this year. He is a heavy drinker and she cannot let him go to hell. And he is a violent man, and a strict man.

Both young women pause, eye to eye, sudden, brimming.

And leaving Vincent will be an agony. And if her dear girlfriend will agree…

The plot is to write to each other every day, just one single important sentence, daily. A challenge. A demand. And for the friend to seal and address and mail an envelope weekly, which will contain Vincent's *billets-doux*.

Now that it is all said, a rosé wine is opened and rain-colored light, a drizzle like vague ghosts at the pane, tops their glasses. Mozart is replaced by Charles Mingus. —I'd be flattered, says the precocious friend.

—You are a blessing and we trust you, says Vincent. His love clasps her friend's hands fervently and the oath is solid. And then she accepts the man's tender kiss on her brow and his whispered loyalty. And she clears the luncheon.

The go-between and the adult agree to meet every Saturday noon, on the wide steps of the Metropolitan Museum of Art. That allows a first hour with the hard, muscled Grecian bodies; she loves to touch the marble; and the second hour with Renaissance lighting on rounded flesh like her own, all before each rendezvous. She will be on the stairs at high noon. And so will Vincent, who smokes a rosewood pipe in the early October-tweed weather. Another perfume to add to her list of details.

—You are a wonderful friend and a dear person. She is dryly kissed on both cheeks again and presented with a small gift and a neatly folded two pages and their unsealed stamped airmail envelope, to which she must add her handwriting and her own words to wrap around the man's, before mailing it off to 32 Fountain View Avenue, Hollywood. She does not open the small, wrapped gift in his presence.

She longs for love letters for the rest of her life. The small gift was Fragonard, which she opened only alone and in the nude and with the lights out.

Her go-between status endured punctually and dramatically for sixteen months. The repetitions were a courtly minuet, unvaried, except that she was only given the perfume the first time, and she only thanked him once. She did not respect the privacy of the folded pages, she read every sentence, she never mentioned her sin or her jealousy, and she mailed them courageously. And she was fiercely proud of her talent as a liar and as a Mata Hari, always wishing for a conversation that would reveal her stolen knowledge. Becoming a different kind of woman, slowly, was her need. She wordlessly waited for the first kiss from the man, which never came.

Once, as she descended the museum stairs for their meeting, she slipped out a camera and knelt like a paparazzi to snap his waiting pose, there at the base. He never kissed her, but that afternoon, in the covert shadowlands of a warm, pre-autumnal Central Park, she photographed him like the Grecian statues she appreciated. —I want to see all of you, she'd seduced.

Conscience-chilled, he sent her home, and then both were mute; and both returned to the steps, on following Saturdays.

A small glossy print went inside her letter. And by the following winter solstice, she received an envelope with no words but a terrible photograph of her friend's face, bruised. The return address was on Fountain View Avenue. The Hollywood father had discovered them, and this was his message. None of her letters were ever again answered. There would be no more envelopes and no more museum steps and each one had a shattered spirit. Vincent brought nothing to the last rendezvous and he said almost nothing. The silence on the steps was all each one mastered. Pipe tobacco stained the corners of his mouth at the beard line. She noticed the smell of garlic. She never wrote him the letter she rehearsed. She never had an address.

In twenty years, a tall woman tracks down her oldest childhood friend. The other, still round, takes tranquilizers before the lunch she has stupidly agreed to. They meet in an open air café on La Cienega, a hint of winter in the California shine.

They light each other's cigarettes. Each has a different brand. Neither one has an initialed case anymore. There is no single sentence, no one place to begin.

A manicured hand reaches carefully for the one whose nails are bitten to raw skin. We each…

She tries again.

…It was the first of almost everything. And it was my first real mistake.

Bruised ghosts. A quiet that frightens each.

•

She returns to the city where she was born. She orders frogs' legs.
It is her second taste.

"Stand still like the hummingbird"

—Henry Miller

Small Craft

He has an impressive collection of Mickey Mouse memorabilia, a lamp that dances and glows lowly in the dark. In the morning he is up and out jogging faster than Bugs Bunny.

—You can have a quickie sauna before ya leave, he calls from the coffeemaker.

He's a baby-faced, six-foot blond, tight belt over a thin waist, small hands. She clocks how he scratches at his hands. Often. An early psoriasis.

She has been lying in his ship-shaped bed, still, not yet able to move after he has risen. She's counting, just how many Mickey mice.

His coffee tastes like chocolate and cherry. At his garage door, he nods vaguely, finishing his juice. —It's good for you, kid, this is a big town. You're a little svelte part of it. She snaps a gardenia from his bush on the way to her car. Shakes it hard, to get rid of its tiny ants. Leaves it on her dashboard until it stinks.

When he came late to their hookup at the old Brown Derby last night, the actress had been waiting for an hour. While being noticed. Only her pumping crossed leg, right knee crossed over left, and that leg pumping, pumping, pumping, showed the banal rage. Nervous, facing the room nearly expressionless and superbly dressed, sitting tight, she kept moving. He answered his calls first, table phone and waiter, both ready. Then he ordered oversized scampi and St. Emilion, a small left hand perching at her now unseen and now quieted knee, under the table; and a lazy invite to his Mulholland bedroom. Just follow him up the glittered drive.

There are no small roles, only small actors, so they said; a given, of the art that makes stars and embers and coals, of starved-to-be-noticed talents. She is un-discovered, she can cry on cue, and has memorized sonnets to prove her worth to gods. She tells no one how she devours bags of Mrs. Field's cookies on freeway drives home from producers' chairs; she looks good in denim shorts and high heels. Her agent compares her to a dark young Salomé when he sells her, one 'a the four great actresses in town, he says. She tries to be big about it, she is just not famous.

—I have a date with a Mister Big, she had crowed two days ago, like her Santa Rosa uncle's best fighting cock.

And her agent rose from his facing black leather office couch. —Just be the best lay he's ever had. And he patted her shorts.

She wasn't.

It's now a private conference. —Someday, darlin', maybe think about a teeny lift? You have the legs. You look great, but hey.

She didn't.

A pebble. A small craft in a nasty sea. She wants a win, before she hits twenty-five. She works out like a fighter. Memorizes and rehearses like an ancient orator: Demosthenes with little stones in her mouth. She refuses to be a lightweight. She wants to be an old-fashioned, new knockout.

There is a very small role. A crazy-patient in a film-noir about locked-up visionaries. The lead is possessed by Blakeian angels, the script is a gem.

Festivals. A guarantee.

She is to sit on the floor of a hospital and draw with crayons, while the lead has one of her best scenes. There is to be a single close-up of her twisted soul which she has let show with all the veracity and intuition she has for madness. She is memorizing Ophelia now. What actress in town does not have frenzy and a twisted psyche to survive the black weather that comes in the sunshine. They are filming in an abandoned former mental hospital condemned for earthquake insta-bilities. The production has a special-use permit for six days before the bulldozers that will come to reshape Sepulveda.

They have been shooting from every angle, cracking already fis-sured and grimed windows and shooting through the new fissures for effects, re-taking for low-flying planes that ruin the soundtracks, re-taking for the fragile lead's upset stomach. Re-taking for unwanted shadows and lunch breaks. It is the long detail-ridden business of movie-making.

The actress with her small role is piling up pages of German Expressionist crayoned faces, on the floor, in take after take. She was always a doodler. She has invented her inner scenario—she is a round-the-bend genius reduced to scribbling portraits of all her fellow patients—drawing furiously, when the camera is rolling, and for the hell of it, during the breaks and set-ups, too. She's ferociously into it. She wears a stained red rayon bathrobe in the scene, and she sits on the linoleum, legs spread wide open like a child playing jacks.

She concentrates with tongue between teeth and one fist clenched. She allows herself to think outrageous and grotesque pictures while the camera rolls. Maybe she is stealing the scene.

Space seems inhabited, to her. She is staring at crying women. Moaning corridors. Foul odors. Sorrows, growls, like someone fastened to a wall like a beast. Maybe she's done too much research. But she can swear she feels them all around, all the former patients in these real walls. Revenants. The place is swarming. She focuses on her crayons.

The director wants improvisation. They have been shooting this take as a long-shot group scene, and her director has taken notice of her, particularly. He signals the handheld camera to pull in toward her, to shoot not her, but the splay of wild faces she has drawn and which are now like scattered rags all around her. When he calls —Cut, he comes to kneel close beside her and speaks so softly no one but she can hear. —You're very good.

She eases back to the hot klieg lights. Receding demons. Real hospital, plaster peeling. —We can't use the footage, he keeps on whispering. It's too dramatic. But someday you'll get on a map, honey. He winks at her and he's off, and it's another dinner break, be back at seven, the outdoor light will be lower at the barred windows. She's still on call, they'll be shooting over her shoulder, from the back. Going into overtime.

Neither flattered by the directorial whisper, nor completely unleashed from the inner, she gulps and splashes chill hospital tap water and its rust, like a parched dog at a puddle. Speeds out of the red bathrobe and into jeans and a tank and she is halfway down to the beach access before she's stopped shouting fuck you, fuck you, fuck you. Her yellow '79 Honda windows all rolled up, sweat sprouting like a rash from all her pores.

She swerves into the parking lot, slams out and is in full-tilt jog down to the hard sand and a long low tide, spit out of her own head/ jog two three four/ jog two three four/ jog/ jog/jog/jog/ the brackish air and her sweat-mix cools her, eyes focusing, still muttering, fuck two three four/ fuck two three four/ jog/ jog/ jog.

There's a sand-slapping replica, just behind her, her own rhythm just behind her, or is it just ahead and coming at her, or in tandem. Or— And then she sees the male in somber-colored shorts, his large hands like shovels. Jagged as rocks-in-a-desert bones. Long heavy bones. Imperfection made with rough crayon lines, long hair, shaggy and clever-eyed, an alert animal. They are running, side to side. I have a radar, she likes to brag. I can find the one in a billion, just give me a minute. They were now a jogging duet and had not spoken; there was no need.

It takes six more minutes to still wordlessly lie down under the Santa Monica Pier pilings, no one near, tide out. Goodness had nothing to do with it.

If they'd known one another at all, the actress might have quoted the Mae West line and they both might have laughed in the middle. Instead, they photo-finish, and she is gathering to her knees to drawl in a low husk —I'm really sorry. I have to get back up to the mental hospital, up on Sepulveda. No one knows I'm gone. She says it deadpan.

She's standing, still as a hummingbird, and remains only long enough to clock the wild man's face change to freaked, and she's gone and sprinting to her Honda. Key in. Turned an inch, she can see the stranger running away, stag, toward an orange and blood sky. —I may be no star but I'm good! She is screaming at the empty parking stalls. Tomorrow she will break all her own windows with her hands. A small craft made of skin in a tidal wave. But now, she is calmed. She drives back to finish the night, windows rolled down. Speeding. Windy.

They shoot low and over her shoulder from the back. The director ignores her. She ignores herself. She draws a very small skeleton, fills her paper with its tiny duplicates, until he calls —Cut.

For Flame and Irresistible

A boy with a cart is giving away cut branches, their exciting adolescent eruptions of unopened blossom pink, oh, I desire one. & I desire me. & I want to know that woman, Tandy.

Tandy was / is / was / is giving away her flaming copper locks, all her opened blossom pink, always did, always will, but no one's buying. Into the tender erotic saleable defended shine of passed-by-now like second-round marked-down maybe scuffed spike heels &

fading eye-bright, her tight pants stand. High, or ugly, or don't-get-fat-now, do-it-drums, perfumed, in all her creases.

No one's buying. The powder breath & push-ups mirror-punched to hot & out-there scary baby—isn't working.

Singing? Her shoulders stiffen elegance into an alto-lyric blue-hour star, before she wanders. Keep me company? she says. Are my pants wrinkled? she says. You're gorgeous, she says. Sing with me?

Well I want to tell her some about my own pink. A woman like her who knows some everything. A woman of the tempting kind, round heeled, old soul woman, you must-have-been-has-been-used-&-sperm-sheathed-silk-for-skin, high-cheeked & freckle-feisty low-growl mama-woman—all jaguar bitch, smiling, & me a wannabe movie star, out cruising, hey! She says come on over.

Then I let me entertain Tandy in her own kitchen where—we're waiting for her son she's taught to please women, she says—the way only a mother who was astro-paid & dazzle-gorgeous can, she says. She's headed in her mirror like a bath. A diver for scars. & lines. & lips. To pass the waiting, I'll tell her all my Hollywood career, all my kindergarten sins. She does not love her wrinkled echo. You're beautiful, relax, she says. Be careful, she says. My son's gonna love you, she says. She likes me. Her son might like—enjoy me. Tandy and her smooth-skinned stud, we're so Venice Beach, see.

When I was twelve & had just grown tits, I tell her—it's my story of a summer on a shining hill, how I humped a boy my age on a bus & no one knew, & not my mother. I want to make the once-upon-a-gorgeous-whore laugh. Like me. Teach me what Hollywood can't, I'm a seeker of, a vagrant of, a woman trying to figure it out—how to be a wild woman. How to be a woman.

How, wide-hipped under my new breasts then, knife-waist, then, I was the blonde in a bus-crowd of black-eyed man-bats. Bodies packed like plumped fowl for the block. How our necks strained over a little air & the nipples of the mountains, how at road-curve speed, my own breasts nested, the boy & I noticed, adjusted by millimeters, nowhere to go. How he wore cotton shorts & I, a yellow dress, & the two of us studied him, swelled; near-wings; how somewhere on that bus was my mother.

This, I love, she says, her unlaced drug done like other women's diamond pins, all spread. Talk about *me*, she says, powdering, for cover. Then we cry.

I vamp until her son comes home & I can / will have him dimpled in the red room, in the seashell iridescence, in the moon's hot silent thighs, I'm thinking.

Patience, darlin'. *Patience is a virtue, possess it if you can, it's seldom inna woman, & never inna man.* I've dared—I tell her—I've swum in oceans that could kill me, I tell her, climbed that black-eyed bat-boy on a bus, once, is she impressed? She's stirring coffee with a feather.

The window has its dealer & his shadow. It smells all California-night-sage. In their house, it smells of woman. Her silk-screened robe's open dragons bare the same shiny as her flame-long waves— but they streak down strands of sadder grey. Her legs hang easy-dangling, freckled ankles, high-heel-smeared. Know how many teeth have circled her strutting?

Am I tired? Tandy, who has done it all, could scream. JFK and Sammy Davis had her red hair in their fingers. She's peeling grape skins. How high a tag her daughter gets, how *chic* you have to—how muscled *chic* & how goddamn street-treat dazzling! Well what if I'm not? *I'm not.* But I'll get whales tonight, watch & see, sweetie. Whales! So maybe they'd rather have, but lookit' how they always tongue her flaming, how they always say, you're the only, only Tandy & she twitch-shine shows her teeth that—she struts her thin tall hips that— her sharp pink knees that—wiggle until they love her. Only sad she isn't quite, so maybe not as—maybe more like—But Tandy! No one's screaming. Only Tandy. Jesus.

She coulda-been a would-be movie star like me, no, lookit', this was way more joy. Un-pitiful. Did she say how she kidnapped the real Beatles once, to get them on an isle in Fiji? Start a race of new

humans cause lookit' us! Instead they gave her tickets & cold cash—
instead she went to Amsterdam & Monaco & played for a queen &
she promised her kids they'd be a sitcom hit & be stars, & she's back
in Venice Beach, a once upon a Southern gal on welfare has a way to
cut the mustard, darlin'. Yes, she's low on—yes! This perfect-ten red
queen is categorically cashed-out, lookit', the tender saleable erotic &
defended stare, dares saints. Scared?

Passed by, like second-round mark-down so maybe scuff spike
heels, the fade to grim's some sad stuff—sweetie. No one's screaming. Once the only, only, only Tandy was bedded in Monaco! See this
sizzle-smart stare and sunset hair? You just do it like you love it to
death, see, that works, my sweetie.

Who will mother Tandy? —If I never get to toy with her golden
fleshed son—

But now, in the slow screen door, stands a torso who has learned
how number one stands, from his mama. You're irresistible, darlin'.
Come on in. She's ready.

He ignores her. Kneels to me. In the slow black glaze of California star-gate, the red-haired boy can have my soul, my skin, my
money. Kiss me 'til she turns out a bulb, like a movie. He's learned
everything a woman can teach a boy like him, I can tell. Or must I
teach him how to love his mother?

HEART OPEN AS A JAW

Day one again. The discipline of an ex-Marine, orderly and strict; a heart that drum-blasts love, like a boom box, when hers breaks in three.

He has an Indian blanket and a bed roll and he always carries a safety pin because his grandmother raised him.

He loves chocolate milk and donuts, he expects her to buy them, so she does. He dances like a temple god, body of a yogi, muscle-oiled and tight.

He rolls his own tobacco as though it were a religious ritual and he sings "Amazing Grace," under his breath.

Dances until he sweats like a mountain spring; he pulls his turtleneck off, hairless torso sinewing with praises to Jesus, Allah, and the galaxies; he loves them all.

Dances to whatever's playing, flutes or drums or pipes or bells. And hums The Beatles' "Let It Be." She's humming "Let It Be" too.

He blesses the day. They dance out for hot cocoa, which she pays for, and he preaches the distribution of wealth to street people who walk in the light, the act of loving one's enemies to death, meaning one must recognize darkness and call it by its rightful name.

He knows right and proper action. Community and sharing are right. I Ching yarrow sticks speak changes, and discipleship in a new age is holy as princesses.

He has the healer's touch. He says her heart is in trouble. Use it.

Addicted to his healer hand, she follows him from the Haight to Arizona's Superstition Mountains and back, like a gosling following its mama hour after hour.

—Are you a Jesus freak? He laughs at her. —I suppose.

But he follows her all over San Francisco because she needs saving. Everyone says so. He walks barefoot so she walks barefoot. They walk barefoot and she's supposed to be a witness, a good witness. Watch how magic operates; how he chants *OM* and kneels to draw a circled pentagram in colored chalk on sidewalks, bold letters that say "Love Heals." How people shuffle toward it, to him. Watch the energy, and how it manifests. Feel it, with her opened palms. She watches and wants him to be her healing man with a slow hand meant for her, but he says her obstinacy gives him terrible migraines. She should learn to love the desperate. And control her thoughts.

Her mind is too powerful. It hurts his head. Shift on the heart. Use the heart. Use the heart, it's a muscle. He has rotten teeth.

And eyes that make people follow him. Children. Wonderful women. There are women everywhere. He sleeps with them in his opened bedroll, but not with her. She's supposed to stick to the heart.

She'd sleep like a pup at the foot of the bed or on the rug beside her own bed, even. She does that twice.

Gives away her bed, eyes on the curtains. He says she is learning empathy. And to know the difference between her sex and her soul. In a black and hiding belly of herself, she believes him.

She thinks he knows white magic.

Look how women come to him. How he can roll away pain and astral demons and make evil leave the room without even insisting. He says he has a job, he's sweeping up the astral.

Look how her heart is open as a jaw, so hungry around him. How he makes things happen. Music stops, or starts; stations play the exact and very words he's speaking. He says it's all love; love heals. Children cuddle to him like Franciscan sparrows.

—Are you like a saint? He laughs. He says she has a lot to learn. He says everything attracts itself. Love. She says —Love me. He says —Learn the difference. She says —I hate you, in an ugly whisper.

He says —You will be blessed. Love. God bless you. Use it. He corrects her. Laughs at her. Says, I do love you. Learn the difference.

She wants to be woman number one but she isn't; never has been. She fakes it, watching him jazz and scat with other ladies. —Sisters. Call them sisters, he says. She smiles like an imitation of him. She has better teeth.

She makes a dramatic show of leaving his fortieth birthday party with a sleek Latin who finds her pretty. —You're a fox, he says against her short hair.

She's ready to follow him into Saturday San Francisco twilight.

A woman has needs. —God bless you, she says on the way out. But she comes back to see the healer Sunday morning; his magnet.

—Chocolate at our usual? As though nothing has happened. He wraps his Indian blanket like a poncho and they hit the street, just the two of them, this once. Cars are honking at them.

—Not at me, at you, he says. Look at the drivers. She looks. Obedient.

—What?

—They like you, he says. They all think you're a fox. A Ford rolls past and the driver is as sleek as her man last night; he's honking Salsa.

—Everything attracts itself, he says. You're wearing the energy you balled last night. She shrugs and feels her chakras clenching. I love you, he says. Her eyes are ash.

Over silent breakfast she sees a man in the grand piano corner who has not stopped staring at her since they came in, he's sleek and when she turns his way he licks his lips. Slowly.

Slowly she turns back to the healer who says nothing and adds two sugars to his hot chocolate. It feels like someone is knifing her spine, it's someone's evil eye.

But she turns genteelly to see the same slick man in the corner, fully masturbating, eyes bright upon her. There's ice in her throat. A vise around her heart muscle.

—Everything attracts itself, says her healer, tamping his tobacco, increasing the weapon's power. Do you get it yet? He leads them out into the traffic. Sunday, leisurely and silent now, no more honking.

Chastised, she's a student of desire. —Use it or lose it, the healer man incants. He switches to "Amazing Grace." Lighten up, sister.

Street people are staring at her. —Somebody offer sister a toke. Somebody does. —Sit, sister. Howz-it? It's Christmas and she has nowhere to be. And they don't care.

She parks on the cement with the street's denizens; she's staring at cement. She's barefoot and she needs a bed and to bathe. She can't seem to move from under the tunnel.

—Use it or lose it, the healer says. He's leaving for Phoenix with another woman. And she has not learned white magic.

TROIKA FOR LOVERS

What she had noticed first was the hump. Then the moist warm eyes and the very high heels that wobbled slightly. Poor woman, she was thinking. But by then the misshapen mother of the man (who had two wives and herself as a pet guest) was kissing her. And she was trying to avoid looking at the woman's large round growth.

He likes Saint Petersburg so much better than the north: that's understandable. —Look at the kind of people he's met. You! Especially you, my *Darogaya*.

Now she was someone's mother's darling. It was going to be a brief Sunday tea. She liked that the man looked like a Mongolian horseman and had a profound sense of freedom.

He came to her in the middle of the night, at first. To be with her alone. He brought a carnation.

The light of a white night dangled like old lace over the city named first for the saint, then for a revolution's mummified leader, and eventually, again, for the saint.

The foreign guest came for the pale nights of summer in Petrograd, she stayed for the snow and her senses.

·

Woman in a window, weren't you part of a Russian ménage during Perestroika? She nods to her soul, which is licking an éclair and hot, sugared chai from the corner of its mouth. Hungry soul. Lover of flesh. Running one finger around an empty porcelain pitcher rim, not willing to abandon any winter sweetness. That was adventure, lady. Old story. The characters might be dead.

·

Gossiping émigrés. She's again at the Café Select on Boulevard Montparnasse at tea time, terrace window. She keeps returning. Is it to hear the language or just to sip in their company? Doesn't matter; she comes. Those from the east have always gathered at The Select, it seems. Russians in Paris, Slavs in Paris, sipping their tea through a cube of sugar clenched between their teeth. Reading newspapers in their childhood alphabets.

·

Three in a bed. Two in a bed. A furred man with wide Mongol eyes and two wives. And her. He'd have set her up in a cabin on a tundra and kissed her into wife number three and come to see her often. And they all lived happily after. Woman in a window, Paris is used to illusion. Russia is not.

It was not Paris she was nodding at. It was suburban Saint Petersburg at the turn of the hourglass from empty to full to empty again. Their time.

That wobbling three-wheeled carriage with snapped spokes repaired for a little while. Like a broken tree branch upheld by a bright crutch. A shutter called Glasnost open to everything not broken yet, and then shut again, and sorry.

The wife with Titian hair urged the guest out onto their fire escape, a tenth-story tenement ledge of a beige, prison-fashion block building from which electricity and shadows played out for miles below. Modernized Russia, enormous body, open as a patient on an operating slab.

—There, the wife proclaimed, like a girl in a pageant, there is my ocean! She shivered and leaned against the guest. She meant space. She meant beauty. She meant paradise. On the bed inside, they were exercising freedom. The guest kept wanting to say: thank you, my darlings, I love this. And, which hand is which? Instead she just laughed with them. Accepted winter flowers. Tea.

—He's the devil, the wife whispered. She had been wife number two since her two small daughters were born; they were asleep now in the apartment upstairs, nestled near the grandmother with her frightening spine.

The wife was brushing her magnificent mane. A cascade in late light. They were all in the slow glow of the land of coital afterwards. Diplomacy. The two women making tea. The man they had just shared and, in principal, shared with wife number one, who was in her own apartment across the Neva River. The man would kiss her later. Now, the man was waiting in their bed beside the fire escape for their return with the stirred chai. All still naked. The women added sweets and vodka to the tray and went back to the bed where he stretched and opened his eyes. —My lovely women.

—No one can say no to him. She was sad but it did not matter to any of them. Russians are emotional. Soulful, that was the cliché. Deep. The guest was observant. And they all lived happily and sadly after.

•

He'd arrive, long-tasting kisses at the diplomatic door; they'd slide toward a worn velvet room and sit like people who talk on sofas for a minute. How hard he worked, when he worked; he was shackled to moonlighting on the Arbat, but here he was. Was she happy to see him? By now his finger would be tracing her neck to her nipple, lackadaisical, and soon he was on the floor and hidden underneath her fabric like a boy under a tablecloth. Of course she dressed for it.

Then he invited her home.

Scratched on the pale green tile wall of their hallway was a bold graffiti: *Soldier of Surrealismus.* —Are you a soldier, she asked?

—Not now.

Everyone wished to know her. Touch her. They were a trio and a quartet and a duet, all at different hours different days. Slow jazz. A man who had survived years before the changes in his country by sleeping all day and staying awake all night. Doing the opposite from his society was survival, its mechanism. That way he might believe he was never a part of the system. That way he was special, had freedom. This was no illusion; it was a tactic; it lasted a little while. The changes only lasted a little while too. A place where people had to believe in something. The guest who pursued experience, who bit the earth like a fruit, who offered optimism as her calling card, she was welcome.

The man who invented his freedom.

Wife number one believed in tolerance. She sang old Piaf songs as though they were new. *"Moi, je ne regrette rien."* She had a dance-hall voice.

Six legs and arms at a time, an integrated single being that had no country and no borders between bodies and no inhibitions. All of their mouths. All of their fingers. All of their sexes. A carousel. An unfinished kind of spider weaving pleasures out of winter thread, sighs out of mixed language and metaphor. *Darogaya. Soldiers of the surreal. Pas de regrets. Cheri.*

Wife number two believed in fate and the devil. The country believed it was on the verge of change. It all lasted for a passionate instant. People weren't dying the way they used to in worse days. People who enjoyed the guest tasted her kind of freedom which had never been theirs. They petted her, gifted her, in order to be remembered. A painted cup. A torn shawl. Their underlined Pushkin. None of them had ever left Russian soil except for off-shore swims in the Baltic.

•

—Why do you like to crawl under my skirt like that? She had a ragged husk of a laugh. She didn't need an answer. She loved it. He must have dreamt of this when he was a little boy, she thought, women visiting his hunched mother and him. Did you hide under the tablecloth and wish? She didn't ask that. A woman knows better than to show what makes her giggle, sometimes. She was just a beloved guest and she loved it. A man, crawling under her skirt.

—No one is jealous, how is that possible? she asked once.

—Are you?

—No. But I have no rights.

—No, said the wife, looking out her window.

—No one does. It's maybe our only freedom.

—Don't leave. Don't ever leave. Everyone loves you.

The mother with her distorted spine loved her. Kissed her and kissed her. The brother loved her. The two wives loved her. Such a time would never come again. She blushed with pleasure. I should die of pleasure if I were any happier. France was very far away.

A troika for lovers, a Russian carriage careening with liberty born of longing, so hot it could thaw ice. Spring before the opened windows all slammed again: a few years of possibility. Night and flowers. The normal snow.

The museums showed émigré exhibits of nudity and borderline porn mixed with iconic Christs and blackened colors, smeared. Vodka was still cheap. One wore the same sweater, the same skirt, daily. Shop shelves were always empty. They were hungry.

●

—I want to take you to a museum, the man announced. Meet me in front. They were a late and dark duet tonight. They moved slowly through the exhibit, more as though it were an aquarium. Abstract paintings by an entire school of émigrés, shown for the first time. And she saw his lips trembling. She reached for his hand and he allowed it. —Will you tell me why?

He turned fully to her, bearish as the cliché, boyish, which he was not. I see the black hole inside my people, he said. And left her standing in the museum.

There was nothing to understand.

The next day the guest walked the river's length. Ice floes, separating. She was a stranger. No longer a guest. A woman in a sarabande that had stopped abruptly as it began. She had no rights. And no right to questions.

●

Woman in a terrace window in an émigré café, someone is looking at you.

What she sees at once is the hump. The very old woman. Then a woman with a cascade of hair, her face buried in her reddened hands. Then, again, the older one. Who is methodically shredding her newspaper whose huge headline is mostly visible. Russia's Day of Knowledge. We are a country in the dark.
Night.
Night.
Night.

Animalia

She's young, he's younger. Outside, it is night and spring is deeper and colder than it was yesterday. But the girl wears her tight white tee-shirt, for the sex of it, for bringing on the season, an invocation of magic. Her breasts are so full of rain, and so ready.

Boys always look younger. But on the back bench of the Horse's Tavern in the 6th *arrondissement,* the boy is the teacher. He is teaching her spiked tongue.

These two don't want a bed; they would have to go outside now, and it is dank and raining. They want this long slick bench, this heat, this kissing, this giggled pecking that has a language. Their bench-leather slides against them like melting silver.

The waiter walks past, shoes turned sharply out like platypus fins. He will bring their *vin ordinaire*, in just a little minute, and he toddles away. This splits their childish ribs, and each holds the other's cage, to keep it from breaking. They hook their sneakers around their table-post, to anchor and slither. And they giggle.

For the moment, they are making the older American lady in the far corner laugh out loud. But her laughter is a mime, an exaggerated and densely silent cartoon that she cannot seem to stop. She is remembering the stranger whom she straddled on a dark Air France red-eye, seasons ago. —Didn't you even know him? Her daughter would have asked her. Layla was never a good mother. —No, Polly, she would have said, seriously. No. If I did, I probably wouldn't have done it.

Her breasts are very tender tonight. Too much coffee. Her breasts are descending, aging toward her hands with their perfect red coral manicure.

So the girl is young and the boy is younger. So what? Their sterling tongue-spikes hook and can't be separated for a long minute, they are crying into each other's mouths, metallic, in a silent French. And then they laugh louder, at the lonely wild brunette. —That table, over there, see? A hyena! She's a crazy bitch, like your mother.

Layla is worried, she hopes they don't think she's scorning them, it's so lovely to tempt the small and the irrational, just from her corner. And to laugh. To be so young, so young, so—hurtable. It hurts her, hints at something uncomfortable as springtime's awful April surges. She stands up on her chair. She hears a melody that snaps her fingers, involuntarily, that jerks her waist, her thin shoulders, her arms lift like gull wings, to find the legato of it, then her smooth tailored hips join in. She is slow dancing, now, for the laughter.

The waiter doesn't like it. He appears below her elbow, a firm grasp, and he escorts her out, to the rain. Which has angry wet feet.

•

In the rain, beyond Layla, there is another woman for whom it is so cold tonight. The gargoyles are breathing ice, she sees. The possible dragons of the river and their shape-shifted forms that can deceive children, don't deceive an exhausted rat. Riverine. *Clocharde.*

Not this old one. She knows a shape when she meets it, animal, or fish.

Well, she knows these shapes—and she lifts her chilled pinky finger at them and she wiggles it. *A beau geste.* The rest of her hand is busy holding her black clothing together against a quick dusk.

The pinky. Its single long fingernail. The other nails are broken as she is. But the one nail, pointed, honed, speaks all she can bear to mutter to shapes. It's too cold. She's too tired, she's too angry with the cold. She piles herself up to a standing pose. She rearranges the several shawls to cover her numbed head and her bulk. She is moving her lips without making any words. She cannot be bothered to bend again, and tie her shoes, so she shuffles. Clears her lungs with a dull wet coughing. —You're polluting me, she bellows. This is one of her terrors. Another one is babies, she still remembers their shape, bloated and near, in ugly dreams. And she makes a tangled black path up the Boulevard Saint Michel. Tonight, the university.

Inside the Sorbonne, it is as it has been for centuries, all marble, and a perfume of solidified knowledge, framed.

The ceilings are painted in academic oils, sectioned into histories. They hover over the students, like wide-winged prehistoric birds before they changed into dinosaurs. For years, the students have been angry at all the ordered systems that teach them, yet they compete for diplomas and arousals. Mostly, they are French children, cared for, and a little too intelligent. And their halls smell of long usage, but of kissing, mostly, of woolen overcoats and casually tied *foulards*, of sneakers, of occasional black lace slips, of socks, blue ink, re-used textbooks, and recent sex play.

Here, there are panels for each classical reference. Here are painted savants, moldings, pillared stones. Here are tiers of ascending folding seats, and the attached narrow tables that their fathers also used to note philosophies, and ancient Greek. Here are center podiums, for long, low, precise voices.

•

It is too cold. The angry woman in dark shawls is limping her accustomed route, the air is biting her bare and blistered legs. She does not control her mouth, its moving silent language, its spasms, its clenched oratory. —Anyone can go to the university. Anyone can have a sit on its holy benches. Anyone can listen to warmed-up brains.

Halls and halls are here, brass-engraved signs for Salle Pascal, and Salle Richelieu, and Salle Voltaire, somberly glorified by gilt and dark pine. Stairs that lead everywhere, and are lost in their own corridors, then hide like comic ghosts next to sudden pillars.

Girls couch on their boyfriends' knees, blasé in momentary power, they lean into sidewalls, laconic, in between their classes. Washed cobblestoned inner yards coddle the dawdling hours they pass with grey embraces, especially in winter. They lean back against the laps, the step-loungers, who are always here, who are always lighting new cigarettes for the heat between their fingers. Newly addicted. And stray intellects lean too, rethinking their earlier abilities, their competitions.

Old men come to the amphitheatres, and they keep their overcoats on, and their scarves untied, inside. The rare female lecturer is dynamically aggressive and she wears nylons and tight skirts. There are those who notice all her details, and they are annoyed. There are those who remember their fathers.

•

The cloth *clocharde* doesn't remember all that she can. Not tonight she doesn't. And her right shoe is a huge annoyance but she can't be bothered with it, and the taste at the base of her teeth is as usual, zinc.

She has tasted decent meat on occasion, but not now. Her lips have been less chapped than they are now. Less burnt. Inside, inside, inside—she knows the black of her nudity, climbing. No skin is under there now, she can't ask any more questions, she has this to do, this moving of her dark mass. And this climbing.

The sound of cement drills in the Place de la Sorbonne has stopped for the day, the square being re-cobbled, polished up, the old Paris enduring it. Drill dust lies in thin layers on everything stationary, an archeology waiting for high winds.

She runs her tongue around her tender gums. A black-suited café waiter is standing tilted into his left hip. *Monsieur* is at his glass door. When he finishes a shift at the L'Écritoire, he'll throw his white apron into its bin. She points: animal. She knows his shape. She wags the long pinky, and he doesn't see her, if he did, he could toss some bread at her. She almost barks, then she does not. —Keep it! She's made two words, out loud.

He does hear her. But he won't, can't look at her face, afraid to catch her soul, as though it were a virus. Instead, he goes inside to wash his hands, they smell of everybody's money and soiled dishes. He empties his leather wallet, fantasizes having leisurely sex tonight. Probably, he will, he could bring a cake.

Not tonight, the woman shakes her large, muscled shoulders, not tonight.

She holds one of the shawls under her jutted chin, a caul that has no buttons. She clasps the disordered, collected newspaper pages, pillows that she'll need much later. Her broad face rearranges expressions, and she stares back at him through his café door.

No garbage, thank you very much. She isn't speaking, it is so bitterly cold, her feet are sliced mutton, food is not an option, she whines, very softly, a sound only she knows, it is company.

•

In the Sorbonne lecture hall an American woman settles into a wooden seat as quietly as she can: Layla doesn't want to get kicked out, she won't dance.

This is the university where her father would have come. He would have arrived from the East in the winters before the wars. She feels like Columbus, today, she has discovered it all on her own: landfall. Her father ended up in Philadelphia, instead.

When she was old enough, and he was rich enough, he wanted her to come back here.

—I survived, for you, my darling. Layla went to California instead. Could not trust a Republican, how could she listen? He did not have a daughter who loved him. He warned her, in his vaguely accented English. —A woman without an education isn't worth shit in this world. He made money and left it all to science, and he died in his expensive bed.

Layla didn't curse him, didn't love him. Then she became lost as some women become. She tried Paris. She knows soon, for no reason, she'll be dead.

Sometimes, she dances, embarrassingly, on chairs. She sings to her father. —I'm worth more than you know… She won't sing. Not tonight.

Today she has found the Sorbonne, like a sudden new wall in her own small kitchen. She is surprised to find that no one stops her when she wanders in to the school from the continuous Wednesday rain, long grey coat, dark winter woolens, rimless spectacles, a face like a hunting raven with a good haircut.

She won't laugh. But here, there are beautiful, young and shining kisses in the columned national courtyard. Here they all look so possible. Tonight, maybe. A suggestion to one, a wink, a hint, maybe, tomorrow. Layla tries not to laugh aloud, tries not to attract any useless attention. The perfume of the place is intoxicating, and she feels ferociously reverent.

Layla has not had an education. She could have, but she didn't love her father, and she didn't love his money, and so she didn't. Now she desires unflawed skin and some new idea to stroke like a sharp piece of broken marble that she could touch and touch with her thumb, inside her coat pocket. She's told herself —I'm old enough to have handprints on my heart. She says that, in the dark.

She concentrates. There is a mural, high and in front of the lecture hall she has slipped into. It is a blue and rose-quartz sunset. It is of old sculpture fragments, lying in huge broken pieces, like fallen trees. Their shadows are long with the late light of the day in the painting. Near its center is a tall standing woman with a square jaw and chin-length hair, and a tunic and a veil and her firm upper arms are lifted, and mountains, and iridescence, and antiquity, and an odd sense of humor reigns there.

The artist was giggling at history. Layla is sure of all this, she has a long nose for art, and no language for it. She has not learned one. It was so big, she could say. And that lady, that lady, in chiffon. Layla fingers the sharp stone shard that she has kept as a souvenir from the drilled cobblestones in the street. A chip of it, in her pocket. A reminder. A treasure that she has scored. And cheap.

A brass placard underneath the mural proclaims it. *La Grèce Antique Se Dévoile à l'Architecture.* She considers what that could mean. She's picked up languages just like her souvenir pebbles. French is in her "pocket." She can ululate her "R's." Ancient Greece Se Dévoile. Unveils itself? Unveils to architecture? She isn't sure, but is this art nouveau? Her eye hangs for a minute on the character at the center of the tableau, the de-veiling woman, lifting her layered tunic, the firm arms. Layla is self-conscious about her own flesh, has been for several years now. Aging is an inconvenience. An embarrassment. In her flat, she undresses alone in the dark.

She listens more attentively to the lecture, makes an effort to absorb it, wrap it around herself like old velour. Something new, for tonight.

La Fontaine. The monarchy. La Fontaine was the king's critic. Then, *Maître Corbeau sur un arbre perché, tenait en son bec un fromage...* Master, the Crow, perched upon a tree, held in his beak... a cheese... Monarchy. Emperors. Kings and emperors were not at all the same, the lecturer offers confidently, like a jazz singer on a roll; she knows more than anyone in the room.

Layla settles in. This is the education she has never eaten. Her mouth is all moist.

The *clocharde* opens the same heavy amphitheater door, not carefully, not quietly. She is where she often lands, right here. She looks at no one. A place to come in. She blows the damp out of her sinuses again, she rearranges her uneven weights of plastic and newspaper and cloth, and she scales the incline to a perch on the high far left. She drags her untied shoes. Her body is annoyed and muscle-bound and cold. She aims for a spot by the open square grate in the wall, its heat like a siren to Odysseus in a hurricane.

She settles in there, lowers and twists and wraps and pulls at her head, a turtle retracting. And in a quick while she is a perfectly still, dark hulk, and asleep in the lecture seat. And in minutes, she is snoring, volume up high, and she is sucking heat from the Sorbonne. Her hands go flat against the grate now, as well as her breasts. She is more splayed flesh than woman, more pigeon, crashed flat in mid-dirty-black-flight.

A student is annoyed. Too conscious of her music. It bothers him.

He turns.

—Right out of Victor Hugo, he points at the old bundle, pompously. He has sensitive ears, his father the violinist has always boasted that. He's proud of everything about himself: his grades, his size, his perfect pitch, his clean hands. He takes it on himself to correct the problem. And he approaches the hunkered form. No reaction, so he rousts her, leaning delicately close to her odors in order to whisper, precisely. —It's ok, old woman, for you to rest; we all must. But you do it quietly! He places a thin, clean, white finger to his own mouth that could kiss. You mustn't make that noise like an old bitch.

He straightens his long boy-spine, pleased with what he's done, and she opens just one eye, and casts it on him, malevolent as all that she knows and is too tired to think about tonight. She turns an eye at him that should elicit bleeding palms and saints' stigmata, if the boy were holy and wanted to ricochet her curse. She casts an eye that will not, is not going to, change Paris tonight.

Now the river shifts to accommodate a new generation's skins.

On their thousand stone perches, familiar gargoyles are singing as larks. And morning-birds hesitate, knowing it ought to be night. Students are forgetting what they have learned, just suddenly, tonight. What they know can no longer be the basis for a diploma, no longer of use. And the old woman watches lazily, her lizard-eye resting. For each, an education.

The nearby long-robed mezzos are not the saints, and they are not singing April's beginning, but they are singing. It is the first of April, and cruel after all. Paris is a city of beauty and black ravens, shifting. Paris is a lover, the Seine his semen.

Layla, the woman from California, shifts in her wooden seat across the amphitheater. An idea she cannot locate is breaking a bone inside her skull, a clot of old blood is rushing to find a place to burst, the oncoming hemorrhage is making her want to dance again.

WHITE WINGS THEY NEVER GROW WEARY

The decapitating and bruise-purple sea that hurt them all, swallowed their babies and mothers and wives and hands, has paused. Is full-bellied. Has plenty of new lovers. And its fish are all fat and bloated and fed.

Come, darling, it's all over. Promise.

She listened to the animals, returning. To the breeze, sweet as if nothing else had happened. The tall and firm-footed girl was one of the few left and alive. She had outdistanced the water. And later, she had made her way down past the broken dishes and mirrors and twisted columns and walls and pieces of pieces. She had seen the shoes abandoned. The jasmine-scented prayers.

But she'd never seen a woman who was the color white. She wanted to smell her. Taste her. Maybe kill her. Surely she belonged to the ocean. Surely she was a servant of the fish.

The girl skirted the edges of shadow cast by broken things and sun that had returned with the suffocating heat. When it was dark she crawled inside the tent where the white body lay, its eyes still shut. A woman. The girl fingered the dust where those sandals at the entry had walked.

Word traveled quickly amongst the survivors. The stranger had not risen from her sheet and mosquito net inside the tent. Not for two days. Not for three. Not for four. And the girl continued to hide in cracks and shadow. To finger dust. To fear.

And when her stranger was moved, it was to offer her to the hungry sea. One devil, conquered. More to come.

But the girl had a different idea from the rest.

She climbed to the copper-colored roof of the only building that had survived the tidal wave. And there, shouting, she showed her truer color to the wasteful sky. Then she demanded wings, and pretended.

I could love again, she thought. Or never.

PAS DE DEUX, À TROIS

Ok, blond. Ok, fifty. Ok, an emotional centipede, a poet, a vaga-
bond. Ok, she drinks tea with milk, café au lait, when it doesn't make
her breasts ache. Ok, is homeless in spirit and has a house between
a sleeping volcano and the wind-slapped sea and nowhere—now she
has a pied-à-terre in Paris. Lucky bitch. Wait. Needless. Survivor.
And suckles love like every other human. Meditative. Can sing in an
alto-husk sort of way. Can climb hills. Can speak French very well,

Russian very badly, can say good night in Indonesian, good morning in Tagalog. Can dance a tango, barefoot, worries about her shape, waltzes clumsily. Likes: nakedness, Renoir, early Picasso, late Pinter, late Shakespeare, early W.S. Merwin, nature, beauty, sex, cognac, museums, cello, empty space, solid oak tables, old torqued trees with twisted fattened trunks and dwarf redbirds fighting over high notes, the taste of rain, the taste of sperm, the smell of Eau Sauvage Cologne for Men splashed on her own skin, Fragonard perfume, the smell of darkest red, the smell of praise, bundled wheat, mountains, the cry that might be love, kissing, white silk, walking-boots. There are wiser women. The tests of our faith are like that classic: spin flax into gold, empty thimble-fulls of lakes into thirsty canyons.

I don't know how to control my universe. I'm addicted to hope. I've tried magicians. They disappoint me. They control me. They reject me.

I've been lost, often. I'm a woman who asks. I'm the woman who asks how close is death, how near is God.

•

There: The Pont de l'Alma, where a princess died. There, in that crashed tunnel. Bridge of the soul, I'm walking across you again and again. When I was forty, I threw a pair of green sunglasses into the river here; maybe I would see better without them. I wanted to stay young.

First, I was looking for adventure; then, I was looking for, had been looking for a street that I remembered very well. I thought that I could find a window that hung open in my memory. *O say can you see*, I sang with a little girl's belting basso, from that window. Tanya, my babysitter with carrot-frizz hair, 43 Avenue des Ternes. *Je suis une petite enfant, de bonne figure…si vous voulez m'en donner, une petite pâtisserie…la bonne aventurrr-e…la bonne aventu-uu-re…*five, and singing what I learned in a park. I'm a little girl with a good face, I love bon-bons and jam;

if you'd like to give me a little sweet, what good luck for me, what a good adventure … I play a game with the children in the Tuileries Gardens while Tanya watches and sleeps. She has a huge stomach. Like a statue. Hoop and stick. Hoop and stick, spun through the gardens, I'm five and I'm a good girl, five and somebody loves me, I'm the best find, the milkiest blue pebble in the park, five and the best *Américaine* in town, five and my mommy is late, she has left me alone with the old woman Tanya. Tanya has red frizz for hair and a Russian-accented French, her English is worse, her kitchen smells of liver, smells of onion, her armchair smells of blood-red must and cat. Its rubbed velvet scrapes my naked thighs. There are dark places in her rooms and the boy upstairs plays with a hundred toy artillery men on the stairs between her flat and his own on the *troisième étage*. He visits every day, he wants me to see his soldiers, his men, his guns. Tanya's balcony thrusts from the window on the *deuxième*, I can wait there and hear the ambulances that shrill below, trumpeting, *pahhh-pahhhmmm, pah-pahhhm, pah-pahhhhhmmmmmm*. Tanya sleeps and cooks and sleeps, cooks liver for her cat, I watch her, she is old age. She has a large stomach; my mommy is dressed in her high shoes and thin beige, she is curved, skinny, pretty, she has a big nose, she will come for me, she is late, she will, but she is late. The excitement makes me nervous so I squeeze my bare thighs together and it feels hot and frenzied and I squeeze harder. I want everything. Everything. She hasn't come for me yet. She's late.

Tanya is my sitter, and she's snoring, and the boy upstairs didn't come today, and I play with aloneness like dirt. I touch all the objects in the room, smearing them, and they answer in a foreign language, I don't understand, they feel dumb, dumb, dumb, dumb, I say it aloud, she is dumb, my mother is dumb, I want a sweet I want a hug I want her, dumb, the dish on Tanya's table is empty and she snores. The light at her window is dimming, I scuff my shoes until they scratch one another like enraged cats, I want mommy, Tanya is mumbling words I do not understand. Her voice is a low rasp, she is asleep in her red chair and she is talking, she is growling, she is howling, no no no no no! Take me tooooo, take me pleeeeeease, don't leave me behind take me tooo, don't take them nooooo. Noooooooooo......... I begin to cry and her eyes, huge and wild, are open now and she sees me and grabs me into her soft, into her cries, shhhh, alright, shhhh, alright petit chou, shhh, I had a bad dream, shhh, it happens some times, shhh. But I will not be soothed. I pull from her arms and crash for the balcony window, *O say can you see by the dawn's early light, what so proudly we hailed at the twilight's last gleaming whose broad stripes and bright stars through the perilous fight* ...

—Chou! Chou! Moira, ma petite chou! Tanya is beside me and I kick her away, *bombs bursting in air, gave proof through thenightthatourflagwas stillthere o say does that starspangledbanner yet wa-aave...* I am shouting and singing to the street below that I am an *Américaine* and my mother is late and don't forget me! And Tanya is crazy and she scares me, scares me, scares me, *o say can you see,* I start the song again, and I sing for an hour until the street is all dark and Tanya stands beside me wailing, people on the street look up and do not come, church bells ring, eight, I count eight, and still I sing *And the rockets' red glare, the bombs bursting,* and there is my mother, coming up the Avenue des Ternes, momeeeeeee, I am hanging over the balcony reaching arms to her and she is finally running and finally I can smell her and she lifts and she holds and Tanya is in a crouch in the corner of her room yelling excuse me *Madame,* excuse me please I had a terrible dream and then and then—

—I am so sorry, says my mother, I was unavoidably detained; and then, like a duchess: We won't discuss this anymore. She shoves large paper money into Tanya's lap and she carries me away, singing to me, in French.

•

Her name is not on any door.

Graffiti drips like dark blood from one wall.

I still thought I'd find the window. Ten years ago, I turned left. The numbers were in softer focus, the new prescription sunglasses should have helped but did not. But there was the long vertical sign I expected, a hat store, its case filled with varieties from autumn berets to Holmes' houndstooth check. And there, soft, above the vertical sign, my second-floor window, open. And my breath stammered. She's dead, I thought.

The front door to number 43 also hung open, a slack jaw. Tiles were bruised and stained, the banister wound up five flights, I walked very cautiously, to not squeak the stairs. If she was dead I should not waken afternoon ghosts. Sun made bold squares and triangles on the wall. I scanned the doors like a metal detector. That one. I reached for the smell of steaming artichoke, acid and green, or liver. I could taste a rubbery jello skin as she had served it. She had breasts the size of late ripe melons. My own breasts ache, the time of the month, the coffee, Tanya, good Russian nanny, poor Jew spat out of the mouth of the Holocaust, they didn't want her, they left her behind and she screamed; she gave a child a balcony.

Her name is not on a door.

On the Avenue des Ternes again, busier, more modern, I insist at one more portal. Somewhere here is my school for the fifth term, I kneeled to be confirmed in its courtyard, Catholicism wearing white cotton gloves from the *Printemps* store, and a coronet of artificial white flowers.

That door. None are familiar, and it has to be hiding. Crevice, school, 43, 45, 49, 55. I make an abrupt left into a courtyard that turns into a street running parallel, behind the avenue, a smell of bleached laundry, black coffee.

Graffiti drips like dark blood from one wall. —*Madame*, I question a neighbor, *Madame*, you are a mother here, yes, please, I am looking…there was a *Madame* Tanya. There used to be a school, I went to a small school here, would you know, on this street?

—There is an *École Maternelle* three streets to the right.

—No *Madame*. It was this street.

—Well, I don't know, she says.

—What you look for? He perches on plump thighs, four door-ways to the right. Beside him, suggestive eyes, very round very peacock blue, laugh at me already. I repeat my query.

—I used to, I'm looking for a school I used to attend, I had…my Catholic confirmation there in the courtyard, here, I think. Here.

—I was raised right here, one-hundred meters, the plump one announces. Your school was on Wagram Avenue, not here. He laughs. Why don't you come and have a cognac with us now, first?

—We're nice guys, they tell me. Two men and a cognac. Her name is not on any door. And I cannot find the school.

I smile, I sigh, two guys and a cognac. Or Grand Marnier? Or Sake? Peacock-eyes delivers all three, and we sit at a shined black table and behind it a white upright piano and modern oil canvases, and in every corner are exotic shells and corals. —My collection, he points. I'm Gilles. I've been around the world, the Philippines, Japan, and I love shells, see? See?

—I…I have lived on an island, I say. And so we are friends.

They laugh continuously. They tease about every subject, the plump one's belly size, the choice of drink, the lunch they have just digested, me, but cautiously, politely, *l'école, ma fille!* I join the teasing, I love how quickly we speak, how the words and words tumble crazily and we laugh like friends, at their black glass table. Their house smells modern, clean, like washed shells. I want to touch the shells. Be barefoot in the sand, their pale rug. One of them is wearing fine cologne. —We're not dangerous, they tell me. See, the window is open! Would you like to have dinner with us? We're having Chinese, Jef, he used to own the restaurant next door, until fifteen days ago. That is why he is fat. Now he quit. But so, the food will be good.

—Yes, yes. All right, I will be back.

At eight fifteen I arrive bearing two mangos.

—Did you go all the way to your island for these? Jef kisses my hand. Gilles accepts the fruit. There is something about you. You radiate.

I radiate.

I am Moira, *La belle.* Moira, the beautiful lady.

—Champagne? We have champagne. How do you like the fish? The rice? The wine? Frenchmen? Every item is a pleasure. So, you have no children? How do you find Parisian men? Aren't we the best you've met? How can you have no children? Isn't this *égotiste?* Selfish? What will you have out of life?

—Days…I won't stammer, I won't… Important days.

—And what, after they are gone?

—Nights, I suppose. Poetry. Thank you for asking.

—What are your passions?

—Love, and intellect, I admit.

—Love, what is love? And we all laugh, and it is so serious.

—What are yours? …what are your passions?

—Table football, and calculations, and shells. And women. But after it is over, you know, I basically forget. For a man it is that way, a woman remembers. I remember my daughters, but the women? And his peacock eyes say "jest." Care. Don't be too much of a feminist tonight. Can I bear to play?

The fat one plays his guitar and the music is suddenly heartbreaking. I do not want to weep, so I sing, a Russian song, then a French, and we are, I am, becoming happy; an adventure is gathering, like shells spewed by the sea. A school behind the school I could not find, a *"pas de deux, à trois."* In a little while they ask that we dance, all of us, in the dark, so no one will look in the windows, in the dark, in the songs. I welcome the dark, for shyness. The wine and the sweet cherries in *poire* liqueur swim in my centers and I dance like a princess, and a courtesan, and soon we sing all together and the peacock's voice is a thick liquid honey and he kisses me between songs and the fat one sings at my thigh. *Je ferais le tour du monde, mon manège à moi c'est toi…c'est* *une chanson qui nous ressemble, toi qui m'aimais, moi qui t'aimais…*and one that goes…you tell me that you love the flowers, and yet you cut their stems/ you tell me that you love the fish, and yet you eat them/ you tell me that you love the rain, and yet when it rains you close the window/ so, when you tell me you love me, I am a little bit afraid.

—Now you. They hand me the guitar and as I try to play one song, any song that I can remember, I fail; but they touch us all in the dark and their touch is vanilla and lychee and we like it and it is too late to do anything but remain. I have them both. Dancing. —*C'est la fête de l'école*, Gilles teases, enjoying my waist, it is the school holiday. We will send you a card every year, ok? *alors, la petite fille…*

I am a girl, and a sexy woman, and this is Parisian. Is this the new Paris, I ask, undressed by careful hands.

—No, the old. We smooth the darkness into silks. Beauty and the beast, they are. The one is polished and delicate and light-lipped and curled. His hair slides in my fingers. His eyes are perfect circles, always open; the other is too well-fed, the friend, hirsute, large-shouldered; they are doing this for each other, they have just spent a weekend in the country, they love to eat well, they are Frenchmen, they have had a three-day meal, they tease, and I am the lucky treasure-find, for dessert. They touch me, they touch me, and I quickly love the beauty, and I tolerate his beast, his liquid baritone hums sometimes, and his eyes always waiting in the wings until I should welcome him also. The peacock's gentleness woos me and pleasures me until I accept the two again and again and play with a river and kiss the river, until we all can flood its banks. We are safe.

Gilles kisses my hair when we wake to dawn-light. —Look at this! He is appreciating my body. Look at this, Jef, Jef, wake up, look what we have. Isn't she beautiful? Jef pulls a pillow over his ears, a large curled boy, a plump fetus.

—Oh, oh, you are gold, Gilles strokes me. Café? You are gold, he repeats as I rise and move to their door, a slow exit, night complete. Gold!

It takes good love to make gold. I touch his blue peacock feathers, with an affectionate forefinger, and fall through the mesh, down their stairs. Morning-in-Paris glances at me, unimpressed, and I open my stride to him; Paris is a man too… I embrace him, anyway: long lover, with the river Seine between his thighs. I stop on the Pont de l'Alma. I throw my new sunglasses into the river current, an offering to its gods, its silver demons. I want to see.

I telephone, once. —Gilles, bonjour. Moira, here. So, Gilles, do you ever go out alone? I elude my nervousness, schoolgirl even then…

—Of course, but I go to see my grandmother this weekend, she lives in the country.

—Is she a hundred-years-old?

There is a pause.

—The other night was spectacular, really wonderful. And you played the game really well. There is a second pause. I will call you when I return, ok?

—Yes.

He does not.

Pont de l'Alma, I am not as young, now. The river has had my dark-green glasses for ten years. And the tunnel…has seen so much worse.

The distance mumbles: its stones passing, crossing one another, on the road. There are no-wheres. Everywhere.

Ok, blonde. Ok, fifty.

Ok solo.

PHILOMEL

She arrived on the scene at first light; an animal hunting a familiar scent.

It had begun in an alley after the snow drifts had covered all that was there before last night. In ancient Rome, the central arenas had been strewn with sand, to soak up the blood. Here was a cement sea studded with islands of unknown footsteps. It was only quiet, and white, and secreted.

She wasn't thinking of she-wolves and old legends of this gladiators' city now. Not of wolves. And not of children. And not of their suckling. She was thinking of a man who had been between her legs two nights before. Eager as a poem. Now a snow had covered his last cry and only she could feel it, ramming her. Now the beautiful. Or the blade attached to it. She knew that she would not see him again. And that there was no one to hurt in return. No one to mourn with either.

She permitted herself to accompany his last circle. His walk. His breath, greying under variable stars, dimming. Her eyes on the snow. An exercise, with her breath. To keep it from stuttering. She knelt to the spot and she began gathering fists of the snow into an uncertain, undefined shape at first. She didn't know how to make a golem.

The dark sun rose. After it was built.

And she lay down into its scraped bed.

Still singing. A nightingale with its heart like a cut tongue. Her legs open, pleading.

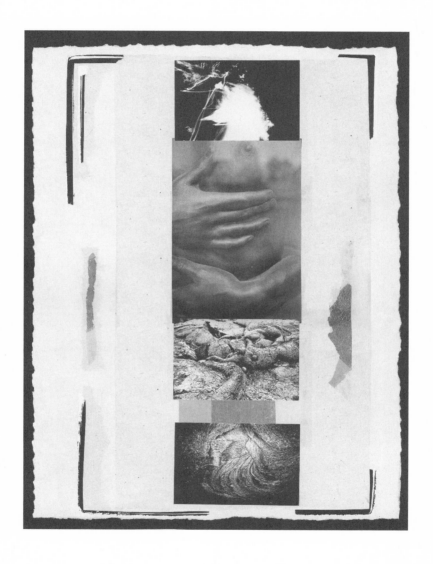

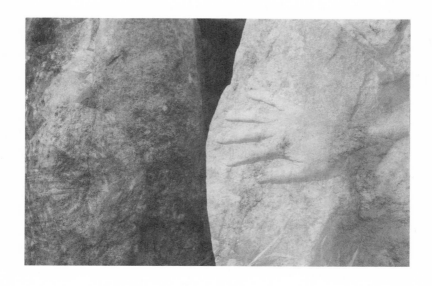

DONKEYS

Sammy had an imagination that could crack eggs, his mama always said.

—You watch, baby, anything, anything you think about really hard—

But she never used to finish that sentence, her voice like crumbling chalk. Sammy could always think of its ending.

Today he was thinking about Siamese twins: a tribe of two. Recent news was rife with it, again. They said only one could live, joined like that.

Which should they allow? Cut. Stitch. One heart. One dead. Think.

Sam and Annie were freaks. The world said so. And they knew it. Being a Siamese twin attached at the heart was like a nuke bomb attached to the pinky finger, just push.

When Amelia held the monstrous birth in her arms she froze. She could make no appropriate sounds. She wanted to growl. But already she had wept, and forced herself to stop it. She clenched her molars. Two little torsos shuddered. Their faces turned blood-clot dark. She looked at them like a cut finger.

When she was a little girl, she had played war with the boys, as soon as she could. She hit one of them with her fists, like she had seen on TV.

Geek. Foreign Siamese geek. The blood leaking from his eye was sticky and orange. She felt terrific; and suddenly she was howling like her heart had exploded.

When her turn had come to stand up for America, there was God, there was a devil, there was Russia, pretty people, and bottled Coke.

—Amelia Flower, please come to the stage to receive your award for good citizenship.

When she got to the part about how happy she was to be born in Bakersfield, and not be an alien Communist, a wave of nausea had risen up in her gut and she clasped a hand over her mouth and ran from the bright stage in sick embarrassment.

Polite applause followed her, and so did the grey Principal. In the wings of the school stage she had gripped her icy fists and gut and decided she wasn't going to get robbed of her moment. She stepped back out.

—I'd like to continue my speech now. My dad is in the army. He defends us. He...

The twins' father was an Army man, too. And he left her.

There he was laid out in his good uniform, holding a USA flag. That's what he wanted. It said so in the will: Don't drape it over; give it to my bones to hold. Life is perfect.

—My country 'tis of thee...sweetlandof liberteeee, of theeeeIsing...Land where my fathers died, land of the pilgrim's pride...from e-e-vree-eee mountain side...l-et... She had to sing it alone, at his funeral, standing there sweating. That was in the will too. She did it with a sweet high voice. The uncles cried. Then she eliminated him from her mind. —Life, she repeated. Life is perfect, she repeated.

Amelia held up the ugly birth in her arms.

The torsos trembled. The place that felt, or the reason their damned-blessed-shrunken soul had a home and breath on earth— the place where they felt, and would feel for as long as their little life lasted—this place—tiny pounding heart, was a bomb. Tick-tick: I want. Tick-tick: I'm pissed. Tick-tick: I'm hungry. They screamed until she stuck her fingers in her ears. She hit her head against the door jamb. Then she got on her scabbed knees.

The scientists knew. The family knew. The infants whom their mother named Sam 'n Annie, two perfect baby bodies attached at one single heart, knew: it was a matter of time. Their plum-sized organ built for pumping blood, knew another thing, a matter of wisdom: once upon a time, not this time, a single heart had been born, and it knew seasons and simple things. How to beat for the horse to run and the jade sparrow to fly. How to call from the cradle for a touch to reassure its question: do you love me? The answer was: Yes, of course. You're one of the tribe.

It knew the seed that poured tenderness as the bellies that made it, thrust; knew peace, in the arms of a beloved, the hope of generation.

It clenched at the cries of a birthing and bleeding mother. It knew old pride: the father who carried his baby; pride in the beast that hauled a plow to till earth where food was born to feed him. The heart was a history, and it knew simpler things: I am me and you are you, and I respect you. There, an April peony, opening its fist. There, a red star. There, trees that my father sawed, that will burn and we may sleep by their heat, protected; or, they may be our house.

History. The heart had legs like an octopus. Cut one off, and it grew back. History: a plane curve formed by a locus of points: griefs, compassions, shames, twisted-up loves, or the tangle of jungles, the implosion of a single flower, the rearing of volcanoes. It knew gifts, and it knew murders. Once, knowing made it healthy. Then it learned to imitate.

—People leave you, 'less they're attached. Hate people like that.

She glared out the window at nearby train tracks.

Those first days after the Sam 'n Annie twins were born were machine-monitored. White-coated minds studied the potential for the attached babies to last another hour. Freaks died, fifty-to-one.

Amelia prayed alternating prayers. Alone as her God-damned God, the daddy gone off on some damn train and eliminated, no right, no wrong, no American way, just a coupl'a donkey-freaks. Her numb brain screamed Odeargod, kill 'em. Please, if you are God, kill 'em because certainly I will, I will, I won't be able to stand this. And then: Dear God, I'm your daughter, I'll be good, I'll be a good girl help me do your will, God, help me please let this thing live, God. It's Your reason. I'm a good girl.

She finally named them: Sam and Annie Flower. The Army man was gone; so no father was going to be named on the science or legal certificates. She demanded that. And one day she carried the terrifying package home, to the room she had made ready for a beautiful and normal baby. The room smelled of lilac deodorizer.

She set to work. She tore apart the good pink crib with her dry-skin hands and got splinters, and she built a huge one. She painted the clean white walls with an elaborate graffiti: For Thine is the Kingdom. For them that are without law, know ye not that ye are the temple. For the body is not one but many. But when that which is perfect is come, then that which is in part shall be done away. And when one member suffers, all the members suffer with it. Over and over she wrote, in fine thin letters: Thy will be done. She knew what was right.

Amelia told people in a chafed murmur —This is my trial. And she clenched her fists until her own long nails pierced her flesh. She fed her twins good wholesome food with a tiny spoon, afraid to break their teeth. She wrapped them in the brightest colors she could find. Purple. Tangerine. Turquoise. Proclaim them to the world, Amen.

Sam and Annie, staring into each other's moss-colored eyes, minute after minute, for years, grimaced; or they smiled, alternately, tolerantly, at each other, most of the time. When their Aunt Sue came to visit on holidays, she was smiling, always smiling; she stroked their small backs with a smooth, flat hand. They liked that touch, and her red hair.

Mama touched just a little. When she played loud rock 'n roll in the afternoons, drinking her Cokes and cognac, they pretended they could dance. She gave them sips, with a straw.

Twisted movements hurt; their small-child grief grew along with their bodies. They whined like wind at a cracked-open window. Amelia whined back at them, after she had her Coke.

There was play-talk; and just sometimes, giggles. —Tell me a secret, Annie would plead. Sam would tell her about the neighbor's terrible cat that could eat up her own black kittens in one swallow; and about Mama's fingernails. They grew in the dark. He told another one. He would swear that their Aunt Sue was taking them away to an ocean that looked like flower-soup, and they were getting real silver bullets, and guns, for Christmas.

—Now you.

—Mama's going to bring us chocolate rabbits with human eyes.

But first she's going to trip on the stairs coming up here. And they would laugh. But so softly. Until she did.

She decided she could educate them. She had kept all of her high-school books in a white plastic garment box. She pulled the books out one at a time, and she read to her children: science experiments, proverbs, histories of the world. Always while sipping her spiked Cokes.

They imitated her diction, which was mixed with her father's philosophies. She pulled out her "Good American" essay, and she read it to them all the way through, uninterrupted by sickness.

Sam said —You're smart, mama. She cried. She said —Thank you, a whisper, to her only son.

Exact mirrors of emotions, when one half was mortified the other one blanched. Once, Uncle Isaac whispered on his way up those stairs —But honey, do you think they even know how ugly they are? Like those donkeys at the fair.

They turned their faces away from each other as far as their short necks permitted. They hissed when he came near.

So love was a surprise.

They woke on a certain morning, in the position their mother's God had condemned them to. They grinned at each other automatically, as their eyes flick-switched to open.

—I bless you. Annie was the first to say it, this day, her voice no more than the usual whisper. —Sam... the nineteen-year-old twin had something on her mind. —Sam... she began, she reached to smooth her brother's black curls with her little finger at the same moment that he decided the absolute truth. He hated her, hated his life, wanted to make her die; and the mother, too, who had been teaching them *the facts*, is what she always called them, *facts, my poor little donkeys, about love.*

—You are here on this earth, God's pathetic freaks, Amelia had warned them day after preaching day, here, little strangers, to show the world that you, who are joined at the heart by a jerk-devil himself who had it in for me, to show the world all about love. She swayed back and forth as she lectured them. —Always, always. God's love. You always remember that. She had said this every day.

Today Sam hated his sister before their mother had a chance to coo her sermon in their ears, voice crumbling. Today he didn't know if he had ever felt just this, but he knew Annie would feel it also. He taught her the impulse, hate, and it scurried like red mites. Electric. They had to feel the same thing, always, in the channel that connected them. Today Sam would not be an example of candy-love. Today, he was male and a passion felt like a hundred-hundred-miles-a-second light, inside. Attached forever to a girl in a position that had only possibilities.

He had thought about it while she slept. Her hands and everything. What they could do.

He pretended, but he had not slept at all, thinking like a twisted wind. Years of words and words about loveandheart and heartandlove and prison at its center. Today, Sam planned. Today, like a cracked egg.

Annie knew right away that there was a chaos that they shared, but it began in him.

Green eyes, unfocusing, the room around them started to fly into storm. When he shut out her face, the flight stopped. He opened and shut them until dizziness swelled, and they saw black, together.

—Don't you hate me, Sam, it hurts.

Her own eyes stung as if the air turned acid.

They lay in the dark and solitary room of the house where Amelia had kept them. She had nourished them, and cleaned them every day, and preached to them, and taught them a kind of survival.

They could get up, damn slowly, and walk sideways like an ancient crab, when it was absolutely necessary. They still pretended that they could dance. Mostly they had lain face to face, getting fatter, uglier, and thought wonderful and terrible things; so much longer than the scientists had prognosticated.

—Sam... Annie spoke to him in their usual whisper, a rasp, one decibel louder than telepathy.

And then he told her everything, and he taught her to want him in the way that he had been planning.

The old house was utter silence, as the earliest dawn light made filaments outside their high window. Their hands were beginning an exploration never permitted, never dreamed.

His breath came as if from the distance. His hands were everywhere. Hers seemed for the first moments to have meditative minds. Then, they wanted to help. They wanted to invent. They wanted to teach a word. And as his adolescence assaulted hers, their inseparable bodies, yet closer, the word spat from her.

Love me, it's all we can do but it has to be that, has to be that, has to, has to, *has to!* Her whisper was turned to owl-screech, as her hips moved. And his.

With her thought, and now with only whatever had made them, that might explain—their heart permitted something new like something bright red and metal-shiny, there in the room with them. It surrounded them, new, like rings around the planets they had only heard of. Wonderful or terrible, it was not the same as their wanting, just a minute before. Wonderful or terrible, it moved in their one heart.

Mama 'Melia's familiar step on the creaking rise to their room brought only a tiniest, hermetic grin, as they smoothed their covers around themselves, and closed their eyes again, pretending sleep. What was tender, hid; and they were touching each other's fingers, under their sheet.

—Good morning my poor donkeys. Amelia drew apart the curtains. Light showed their red swollen mouths.

—Happy Birthday to you, poor darlings. She stood starkly above their bed.

—You were here to show the world, always. She was barely touching her children's black curls. They opened their eyes again and let her see them. Remember that, won't you, as long as you both live? Her eyes were caverns.

Beast-of-burden pale, they arrested her intention. She had meant to relieve their endurance, on this birthday. She had planned it and planned it. Their unquestioning gaze, unbearably mute. Love as obvious as the fact that it was morning stopped her hand.

—We're freaks. Sam chortled as he pronounced it; a word that made him gut-laugh. With explosions of air.

Alien-Com'nist-cap'talist-'Merican-Siamese-freaks!

Annie repeated, and her clattering laugh had no fear in it.

…I can die, Mama. Do it now.

…Freaks, said their mother very softly, laying down the weapon that she was carrying.

Sammy, with his enormous imagination, destroyer of worlds, turned as far as he could… Mama, he said, quiet as the crack of an egg, Mama, I love you, too.

BENCH

The Bois de Boulogne is known for risqué business, orgies, trans-
vestites. Naked men bounding out of summer bushes.

But there in that vast Parisian park, an old man loved Botticelli,
and Reubens, and round-assed women. There, he'd told a girl he
loved like a wild-breathed Artaud, how Versailles was built. How the
women of Paris descended on it, demanding bread, bearing bullets.
An old man visiting a hill he'd privately named for eternity and for

the scorpion. There, he'd cupped everything curved about her.

Now, a boy-grin in his middle seventies, and a persona who waves both arms in the air from across a street to say —Hallloooo, I greet you. A disheveled and casual dresser with an old yellow woolen scarf spun around his neck, and the slender neck is circled under the scarf, with a large white gauze from a recent remove-the-sun-spots-which-could-be-dangerous gouging. It's spring-ish, so he wears the winter coat slung over his shoulders like a nineteenth-century cape, and it keeps slipping off a narrow collarbone. But classy, cool, humorous, distinctly an eye-twinkler. He has a pedant's slow gait that makes those on narrow sidewalks or park paths wait, as he searches his thoughts for the next verse, as he walks. But a poet. An old poet, going back.

Yes, the little bench was there, overhung with more eglantine than when he was young. Highly set on the second sculpted garden tier above Ophelia's weeds, each one named, the rue, the violet, the wild daisies, the fennel, the columbine, the flower whose name he can't remember, the one called dead man's fingers, after the mad scene…all this is the Shakespeare garden of the park he had loved in. He remembers the bench. And Ophelia. On the rotting wood, he had proposed holy rituals for their loving; and as a pacifist, she'd refused a dreaming idealist headed for a war fought by fascists. She thought they had a few months of penniless and sacred sex ahead, she had stolen her parents silverware and slipped the result in his pocket with abandon.

—The garden peony relies on a sugar ant to blossom, he plows in the floral fist to find the sweet he left there, and a ritual commences, a documented marvel of our natures, she told him once. How had she known such botany? He held her black hair as though it were finer than her parent's silver. He held her shape as though he had sculpted its rounds with his own hands.

In love as a mad horse, and she was his darling. (She knew how to undo his belt as though she were arranging flowers. She smelled of vanilla. She never wore perfume. She never wore underwear.) He wanted to take her to the most elegant restaurant for the perfect meal. She wanted to marry. He loved her but cared little for marriage, but if she wanted it…so he bought her a good ring and for a week she wouldn't try it on. He urged her to the Bois de Boulogne, for atmosphere. But the elegant restaurant with its private gazebo, its turn-of-the-century wealth and romance décor, was closed. Just behind it was a small garden that he knew well because he had gone there more than once to make long poems in its viney shadows. It was planted with all the flowers poor mad, poor dying Ophelia enumerates: here's rue for you and some for me… oh poor wretch to her weedy lay. The Shakespeare garden. There, the once-young poet had led his then-reluctant fiancée, and on a delicate bench he delicately pled for her and she mysteriously refused him.

On that bench, he asked again, and settled for her virginity, the restaurant closed, the ring refused.

He tried all that summer to make her more passionate for him, than for a cause. He knew her medicine was abandon. Its rage. She knew his medicine was engagement. Its paradox. Neither saw the mirror in the other; but by then she had said —I can't. By then, he was telephoning her from a cottage in Ronda where there was a statue of the poet Rainer Maria Rilke beneath the square. "…Fling the emptiness out of your arms/ into the spaces we breathe," he quoted and quoted that Germanic poet, who once had come to Spain.

—Come, darling, I have a getaway, we can marry with no one around, come, love. Come. And she said —I can't. Her brother was political. Her brother said —Spain, oh no, that terrible Franco is there. Not a political animal, but an unbroken steed and a philosopher, the poet surrendered the useless ring to the river at last, never able to win any victories for humanity.

The girl married a fellow traveler, had three children and died in a fever, young.

Now, the old yellow-scarved poet has found a charming woman on the metro. Some summer Good-Mornings are meant to be.

No one reaches their age without a past of ragged baggage. They decide to tell one another nothing of any day before they met, today. An aging man, an aging woman, a random blessing. And he takes her to a lovely spot. He has forgotten anything else.

He has pretended to kidnap her, they have laughed, and they have looked at flowers. He has cupped her summer-dressed bare arm, loose flesh; cupped her full hip as they walk, walked with his arm around her shoulder so that his hand can fondle her through a sheer blouse, kissed her with his tongue, eager, insistent; and quoted two of his own poems, nonchalantly. He has taken her to the Bois de Boulogne. Not remembering until memory floods him like a summer rainstorm. And then he is in the middle of an awkward lying, a ridiculous straddling, a petting, a passion on a tiny bench in the garden above mad Ophelia's flowers. On that same frail Shakespeare garden bench. And remembering the girl who stole the silver, stops the symphony…

Now he visits the garden without fail. He hates his sheets. His curtains. His quiet.

"I know this city. The tongue with which its inhabitants fool the sun."

—Pablo Armando Fernandez

CON UN BESO DE AMOR

Yes, I'm going to Cuba. To make erotic photographs. I know it is not comfort; how could I write comfort; what to weave it of? I have no such thread, not now. My world verges on 1939, year after year. There is a Middle East, an American White House with war in its bared teeth, and madmen replicate in every country, like strings of paper-cut dolls. It may get worse. It will. They pretend to be happy? Maybe, they do not pretend, maybe they are singing in their prison camps like the rest of us locked up or not— And music. I didn't fathom how loud. And I hear they dance & dance & dance.

xoxox...

The music is deafening. I'm assigned to illustrate a French woman's erotic storybook. I'll have to shoot backseats, churches, and Lionel's bedroom to find lust, true and construed, in dust-drenched Havana.

I ask everybody what they think erotic is. What makes them want to do it. That's all I learn. The author says she's an expert. A sexologist. I'm a woman with a feisty camera.

—*Suave. Suave* says the man who picks me up in downtown Havana heat, distracts me from photographing bicycle shadows and gates and a sudden white smoke that looks like ghosts.

He takes me to a next-door bar because he hopes to speak to a stranger and I say —Yes, ok, show me. Next we're salsa dancing, and the musicians want a dollar to keep playing, so ok, and my hips work too surely, and I must be shown to dance more slowly, ok, from the belt down, *la cintura, suave, y suave,* ok.

I might have stayed the afternoon if the nice man's hard-on were not so obvious. I am heroically delicate. Middle-aged sophisticate. —This is a privileged moment, I mumble; but it's just a moment, my dear, thank you for the dance.

What else would I say? ok, slide away, looking for the ghosts, *y suave, suave.* But I will wish I danced tango like my sister Kate, while the erotic project pushes most of my buttons: prude, feminist, femme fatale, vagrant, *voyageuse,* so what?

Here I go, I'll never be fifty again. So what. I'll have some buttons. Still I have no thread.

Erotic project?

So there will be naked fat women and voodoo at a distance and a boy with shells implanted in his penis for ladies' pleasure. That's the kind of stories the French lady has written. I'm telling myself it will be marvelous.

The French authoress of erotica gives me a list. She knows people here, and how to take communal taxis and how to buy milk, or bread, or not-yet-rotted *fruta bomba*, pink as an inner-flesh infection.

She gives me instructions for unknown locations and how to pronounce them, which I memorize. She talks about food. The cultivation of taste. I am a hired gun with a single eye. She tells people —These will be artistic, this *chica* is a *fotografa artistica*. Your images are so sensual, so passionate. So "woman." She says they'll all fall in love with me. I don't know. I'm shooting from the hip.

It's the hour between dog and wolf.

A mad *voyant* appears on the rooftop where I am waiting for the couple who've agreed to let me photograph them nude, in tantrified embrace, backlit against the polluted downtown sky; Havana pollution prettifies the sky to that color of the inside flesh of an overripe papaya.

Downstairs, the sister of the man I'm waiting for is having a *Santería* purification ceremony. I am waiting on the roof.

He leads the sister up in white, her newly purified hands high-held; he leads her by one elbow; he walks her round the roof's perimeter, her eyes shut tightly against the light that I am watching like a photographic raptor. Anxious. Perfectionist. These pictures are supposed to be in silhouette and backlit by sunset; I'm losing light, impatient as a cat pretending to be patient. He'll be finished in a moment, be patient. I'm patient. And up comes the *voyant*, in a bug-eyed trance, rattle-cackling like an asthmatic rooster, coconut bowl in one hand, straw hat and staff in the other, just up from the *Santería* rituals one flight down. He explodes through the roof door, spies me and zeros in to cackle-croak at ones I cannot see but he certainly does, a shadow, a shadow, *la sombra*, follows you. I will not tell him that today is the anniversary of my mother's death. That I try the outdistance technique, every year. Don't catch up with me, death baby, I have a little more to stare at.

A bike mechanic watches high-heeled calves, I'll shoot him through his wheels. Next set-up, then the kiss, candle light on the widest angle of a marble staircase, winding.

I lie on my back to get it. Now from the cool floor, I see the columns, the legs, the legs, the hand, the wrap-her-leg-around-his-thigh, the sound of higher, yes kiss her, a little sexier darling, more *sata*. *Sata* is more wild and woolly, more insinuating, yes, you all know what it means. I'm just the foreign photographer.

We do the massage parlor; the angle should capture lace, and his religious beads, peeking. What is that religion? Not exactly Catholic.

They're all dolls and shells, all yellow, blue, red, primary. They'll leave a cake for an offering. A cigar, reddening.

I hear they eviscerate goats. I don't have to see that. Those people in the street who wear white? Are they pure? Oh yes, initiates, yes, pure, must not get caught in rain, must not get dirty.

Do they have sex? This is Cuba, darling.

Don't photograph the white-clad people. I admittedly was trying to take one of the lacy little girl holding her daddy's large hand like a bear's paw; he begs me silently; she's in white. I'm no monster.

Your child is being purified; everything here is crumbling, dust, decaying, a little or a lot. Wearing white is an accomplishment.

At Christmas midnight mass, the cruising boys are making dates; I heard they were tortured. Now they wear tighter transparent tee shirts.

That man, that face, pierced with rings and studs a hundred times or more, lets me near enough to smell his breath. Take one of him at the empty font. Has everyone used up all the holy water?

I pretend I'm photographing the architecture of this nice cathedral. But get the men, the skin, the tight, the bulging, the lean angles of body languages.

We're sleeping where the childless wife hates to cook and has dogs she calls *preciosas*, that she treats like daughters. The revolution took her furniture: old cups, chipped plates, unmatched chairs and chandeliers remain, naked bulbs that Blanche Dubois would hate. Our rooms have beds, sheets, a marble stair to get to them.

The dogs have their own empty marble-walled room, chill, in the sudden nights of shivers. The childless wife is seventy-five, a debutante, once, now, a stained man's shirt and pants on hips grown thick with powdered milk and sweetened coffees. —*I hate to cook*, she says so every day, preparing copious stew for the terriers. —*Only for you, darlings. Sí, mis amores, sí.* Her husband says he does not dance except in bed.

—*Was there any bread today,* he asks? —*Who cares. I hate to eat. I want to go to Varadero and eat only ice cream.* They will not go to Varadero.

Their house, that was their house, is gone, there. Tonight they will sit again as every night, before the TV flicker, not asleep, not awake, in the dark. His button fly, open.

—Get the billion banyan roots. I do. Gnarled arthritic crawling fingers digging in for the endless haul. The long skinny reach. Their hairy fringe, cut shoulder-length, chic.

On every street we walk, their perturbing shadows lengthen. In a rocking chair, yesssss, in the corner so she looks a little swallowed in space. Yessss.

I'm looking for some natural light, I lend her my *pareau* to wrap loosely. —Lower darling, let just the one breast breathe light. Yes. Lovely. Now smile *sata* for me. I give her the wrap. It's Christmas. So this is erotica.

Billboards cry out No to terrorism, and No to war/ Sí por Cuba/ Patria o Muerte/ Cuba Sí—as always/ No force in the world can overcome our resistance/ Nothing is nobler than education, signed, Fidel/ For our revolution of ideas, Dispuestos a continuar/ Always young rebels/ An old age with dignity/ Nothing more noble or human than a school, signed again, Fidel/ Señores imperialistas, no los tenemos absolutamente ningún miedo. Mister imperialists, we have absolutely no fear. Cuba Si, Yankee No, in yellow, on the playground fence./ Our revolution is a flame in the eye of the world./ Together, let us fight for a better world.

—Dead like a dog, buried like a hero, says the childless wife. We are drinking her hoarded coffee. There won't be much else to eat.

She repeats —*Dead like a dog. Buried like a hero.* A dictator can kill his best friend. Did. Eyes can be gouged. Were.

—Get Lionel searching in the vanity mirror, oval framed in tiny candle-watts, one bulb, suggestively burned out. Is this artistic enough?

—Lean forward, Lionel, as if you could tongue the boy you are in the glass. Yesssss. Yesss. He does. In fact he dances for me in the doorframe, not erect, but ready—his large hands, his nakedness, silhouetted once again for art's sake.

He bows for me like a master of ceremonies, welcome in. Oh, open, my heart. There's no one on the surface. Go in.

Madame Erotica seems huffy today. I call her on it. —Yes, she admits. I scratch like a cat. Just keep shooting.

All the women here know low-cut and tight. Just keep doing Salsa, but *suave*, from the belt, music loud enough to cover the unpleasurable. It's hard to make it look like they're flirting, and there is never enough light.

Use the long aperture on the widest lens, make everything look attenuated, wide. Yes slightly distorted, yes it's an Alice-through-the-looking-glass kind of place. Everything is always "else," reversed.

Check the jazz. The dread-locked dying angel who plays three trumpets, stoned. The saxophonist, a cheek swollen with a high note, bulging.

The fat woman has too many scars; oh, breast reduction? Don't tell me. This one is not pretty. She's a hard-jawed lesbian and she's getting excited posing for these pictures; I'm not; don't kiss me good-bye on the lips please. I'm still a prude shooting erotica. Forgive me.

The story I invent: a couple lounged in the backseat of a '54 Chevy, in the land of after-sex "afterwards," she, smoking a fat cigar. The expert author is pleased; the erotic project is progressing.

—Wear the black, low-cut and bustled, says *Madame* Erotica. She wants to be in charge. I'm dressing up for them now. Crawling on the floor to get my angles.

But I am loved, for making imaginary pictures they have never seen. They blow me kisses. They perform for me. They want me to love them too. So I do.

For one night, I watch, without a camera. A marble-glowed interior, the chandeliers' dusky gleam. I'm getting tired of being a heroine. Someone, dance with me for real. —Please?

Outside, there is a parked red Chevy. Forget my heart, I'm here to work. I grab the Nikon, send the tall turbaned girl into the backseat with a posed lover.

—Smoke a cigar, darling. Here. Not him. You. She lights it like an executive.

On the Malecon, under full moonbright, a lone pescador in his rubber raft is tying on a day-glow scarf and vest. The tide is rising, tomorrow's storm will compete with the pull of the moon. This night the band of serenading guitars are tin-eared and earnest. They want/need/want/need dollars.

Next year dollars will be forbidden once again. I follow the man and his raft with only my eyes, his uncles or his cousins or lovers who once escaped in worse boats, or died trying.

With this open sea and this open moon, he will not go very far, that's against the law. Once, good people or bad people, depending on the view, ate prison soup or were blinded or scarred, here, or prevented, or revolutionized into good, or changed into silent humans, here. Saved, and the gnarled digits of the banyan roots reached nearer their homes with marble pillars, naked statues, memories of American educations and dresses from France.

On their thin fingers, they are counting bread rations. Skinny dogs, killing each other, but escaping speedy vehicles. Long shadows, escaping their ragged trees. Columns, like women who never had to cook, decay today like unsuccessful overthrows of greed: this too, is called a revolution.

This isle of sugar and figs and hawks. This isle of difficult lives, pedaling uphill. These hawks, concerned with wind.

This island of bruised pieces, call them flesh, call them statues of the questions, call them lives.

This island of anthills making music loud enough to drown out the annoyance of sorrow. And I am making pictures of breasts and rounded butts and brown faces.

And I who hate heroism as they hate Yankees, who cannot really understand the slogan *"Patria O Muerte,"* because I so disagree with dying for causes, I am making pictures to compete with global blindness. Mine.

Patience for less and less perfection stretches like a girdle over highs. I am strangling slowly, and I am doing my job, making the pictures as I go.

Bring chocolate, *Con un beso de amor,* with a kiss of love. Electric-as though ghosts teased the houses. No water today?

of captured liquids, clean and filthy. I have come to one rld. Where they wanted to change mankind.

ag said in her *I, etcetera,* she travels to see the beauti-good-bye to them. I traveled because I was going to make erotica.

Not sexual tourism. So I loved them with my lens: *preciosas.* Until I lost the light.

I am afraid that I won't go home. And then I'm afraid that I will.

"It is at night that faith in light is admirable."

—*Edmond Rostand,* Chantecler.

LE SERVEUR

The city is a lover with the dragon-river running like a golden mud between his long thighs, that's how Louise sees it, and has since she first fell in love with Paris. And her other lovers are fewer than they were, by far.

The skies are colored plasma and gunmetal. And there's another war. It's good to see her old friend.

—Francesca, your hair is lighter. Louise, stop crying, it's only life.

They're out in the late March-chill rains and have watched a tragic movie. How men are. How they lose their minds. Tragic soldier bludgeon-kills his Kandahar prison mate to save his own ferocious ambivalent life. The wife will never have the man who left her sheet, again. Now he's a killer.

—What kind of men can we have? At our age we better giggle about sex instead. And Jesus, when will it be spring?

And then they can't speak. And then they can't stop. Wars. How will we ever not all be murderers? Men, what men we have left.

—Laugh, Francesca insists, laugh so it hurts. They're cold. The sky is the color of global rust.

Movie-ing with a henna-bright-haired Francesca who's shown up again in Paris, who always has a lover in every port and always says she's just a Viennese courtesan at heart, batting her crease-framed turquoise blues, smiling more widely than most women do. Her teeth demand space, her bravado a little more, so her smile widens, and widens. Francesca, who can always get some male to carry her heavy packages, fix her sink, catch and sweep dead rats, adore her with spring flowers hung on her doorknob with love notes until the next one steps on that one's cuffs. —I've never been single for more than a month, she shrugs, and Louise knows it's true, how in hell does she do it? It's not the brightened hair, it's not the generous hips. An earthen-voiced-cynic-scholar who never gets out of sweatpants and turtlenecks and nylon layers and expensive black sneakers and a silver necklace and always notes Louise's low-cut everything, whatever she happens to be wearing. Francesca has just had hip surgery, so they stroll in the early darkness, like snails, with a turquoise shared umbrella.

—Men… they can't stop… Cannon fodder… My country…

—My sea-sick loneliness, Louise says, as though it could be for a laugh.

—Wine at the Café Rostand? Grand old setting named for that dramatist who invented Cyrano's love letters, and facing the high black iron fence of the garden of the Luxembourg. Ecstatic Medici lovers and stone angels and pre-spring infant-size erection buds, on the lindens and future cherry trees that are not flowering yet. It is still dank, and March. All the garden's marble-carved passion is locked in for the night.

—I hate the nights. I hate the war. I hate us, sometimes. They agree. They want to drink. Wear off the film. Wear off the war. Francesca is warming up, her massive hands draw circles within circles on the table. She's tipsy-crowing, her charm-voice is lowering. She's a save-the-last-gasping-globe-activist in Hartford, her famed-intellect father who died at ninety-seven, last month, after a very good life, left her free fame points; so she stormed her senator to shame him for permitting the newest about-to-be nuclear pad in the Northeast. But she could see "she's a dog" written on the good senator's forehead in transparent ink.

—What's that mean? Well, that I'm not so gorgeous and so he hopes I'll say my piece and get out of his office so he can flirt with someone hotter after his long congressional day. Thank God I had my George to go home to and go to bed with. Louise looks carefully at her. Fluffed colored hair, paler and more silk-conditioned than the last time, same sweat pants, wily old Viennese stare and the counting-details courtesan-eyes, the crone's black humor parting her lips. —You're a Russian tragedienne, she taunts her friend. Laugh, she prompts. Yes, there's always another war.

So they're café-sipping Sancerre to ward off Francesca's advancing migraine, Bordeaux to flush Louise's cheeks. They toast, slowly. To men. To women of a certain age. To sex. To the goddamned country. The waiter is bite-the-fist-young. Young and morosely frowning. Are those thumb-sized dimples? Curly forelocks, bone-slim hips and a sourpuss face. Louise performs her best mezzo-register-French. —Having a bad day? *Pauvre chou.* He switches masks in a rooster's heartbeat minute, dips over the table and kisses her on each bright cheek. —*Ok! On fait la bise,* he crackles like red cellophane. Bows, like tall summer grass.

A nice auntie? His new mama? Just who is she, here? —Now I'm having a good day, he swaggers. He's off to get their sizzled black mushroom omelet. He returns and returns again with fresh napkins, spoons they do not need, coffee, a bigger wiggle to his walk and then a wink and then a purr and then a quick dip for two more kisses on each of her reddening cheeks. It's getting honey-sweet and giggly; he's twenty-five, maybe. Maybe.

The women *gotta pee*. Down the winding Rostand stairs to the ochre-marbled *Dames*, they haven't gotten down to brass-tack-talk yet since their last, a year ago when Francesca smoked it out of her. Yes, she'd even once stepped in and had a testing conversation with a Montparnassian marriage broker, —Oh, Francesca trilled. One of her most beloved of the men-in-every-port, a gone-astray-for-the-courtesan-bishop who brings her posies and lead-weight-guilt and beds her before Mass, but never after...well his sister went to one of those, and now she's happily wed. Very Parisian. Her friend wants all her details. Now.

Not much to say, a grimace into the silvered ladies' room mirror, brushing out her winter-static straight blond. Three old goats who live with their mothers and are balding and think she's really quite unusual, poetic, in fact, too unusual for them. The broker who had the small size of Jesus' sculpted clay hands on her desk and said she'd call when she had someone, hasn't, end of story. Louise is readjusting her black leather pants.

The ladies room door swings wide and there's the waiter, he's followed them down, he's smiling like a lean curly sparrow-catcher, about to pounce, unafraid of the pestilent avian flu. He sweeps in and now he brushes Francesca on both cheeks and then, no preamble, nothing, plants a spring garden of a long kiss, moist mouth to Louise's, flower after flower, and does not stop and does not stop and she's far too surprised to stop yet, and she hears the other woman say —Well, I'm leaving now. She says it twice. He keeps kissing and she keeps being surprised, the other one's gone, and he's pulling her left arm toward one of the cubicles. —That's it. No, darling boy, I don't do tawdry. No. That's not a pretty enough place for me. He perfectly understands her French.

—Later? —*Pas ce soir*, she's treading womanly waters here. —But soon? Soon? —What's your name? He tells her earlobe —*Jean-François.* His hands butterfly-skim her sweater, does she understand correctly the mumble that says —*Jewels, these are jewels, please, will you give me your number?* He's darting into the cubicle solo, his one hand reaching out like a silken paw for her number just as they hear the outer door opening and a proper café-denizen-dame is heading in, they hear her high heels clicking the stairs, and he has kept his cubicle a millimeter ajar. In an intrepid daze Louise scribbles her portable phone digits on a ripped paper towel bit, slips it into the slat and is gone past the clicking high-heeled, black-net-hosed woman heading down; and she's up the stairs, and Francesca is above, demurely welcoming, hands spread wide like tarot cards on the table top, as she lands.

—That man over there, Francesca points to a superbly handsome age-appropriate person in the other corner. He's been flirting with me over your shoulder the whole time we were sitting here, you know, he just walked over and he gave me his card while you were busy down there. Nice time? Well of course he's smitten, you're gorgeous, gorgeous, she applauds. Ah, she sighs, it's good to be back in Paris.

Louise's portable phone rings. —*Oui?*

—*C'est le serveur, Madame.* It's the waiter, she knows, she knows. He's a free gift of Uranus, planet of the un-expectable. It's Friday night. It's ten o'clock —*When can I see you?* She hears an echo, is he calling from the kitchen or another marbled cubicle, or the twisting stair? —Ahhhhhhhhhh, Monday? she stalls. *Lundi?* Monday. She could not bring him home to her cat, could she? Could she book a three-star-room with a balcony? The website astrologer has mentioned that her sign has climbed to Uranus, it's a reckless cycle for the unanticipated, now she remembers, don't be amazed. For tonight, the statues behind the Luxembourg garden fence are having orgasms in the cold; and she's been carrying this printout novena offered by the Church of the Miraculous on La Rue du Bac, in her purse all week:

To St. Raphael, Angel of Happy Meetings & Catholic Singles: O Raphael, lead us towards those we are waiting for, those who are waiting for us! Raphael, Angel of Happy Meetings and Catholic singles, lead us by the hand towards those we are looking for! May all our movements, all their movements, be guided by your Light and transfigured by your Joy. Angel Guide of Tobias, lay the request we now address to you at the feet of Him on whose unveiled Face you are privileged to gaze. Lonely and tired, crushed by the separations and sorrows of earth, we feel the need of calling to you and of pleading for the protection of your wings, so that we may not be as strangers in the Province of Joy, all ignorant of the concerns of our country. Remember the weak, you who are strong—you whose home lies beyond the region of thunder, in a land that is always peaceful, always serene, and bright with the resplendent glory of God. Amen.

Other women say they've had miracles.

On Saturday he called only to hear her voice. Whispering, charmed, she protested, she was occupied for the weekend, but she repeated *—Lundi! Bonne soirée.* Sunday he sent a midnight text to her telephone spelling *Bonne nuit,* unsigned. She had now become the patient one, about to pounce. Monday, he regretted that he must work late. She, that the hour was *—Oui,* late to begin an evening, later, midweek, perhaps? *—Oui!* he promised, *oui!* Thursday, she lit candles and stopped waiting for the rendezvous that did not blow the candles out. Or for Uranus that served the undependable, for faith in light.

Francesca said —Stop it. Just stop it. Men can be like that. Yes, no, maybe. So what? A pick-me-up. You needed a little lift, Louise, yes? I made it happen. I'm your damned fairy godmother, say thank you. And don't be tragic. Louise slouched. Sit up, Francesca demanded. Louise practiced nonchalance.

She returned to the Café Rostand once, alone, where a waiter had boldly kissed her senseless until she had imagined him a true gift of Uranus, or the Lady of the Miraculous Medal. It being Paris. Did he do that often? All the time? Was another woman more of a lady, and had that one confessed to the manager and had him banished to the land of impulsive dimpled boys? None of the waiters was the boy who'd served her. He'd tried it on someone else and been fired. Or broken his foot or his mind on the metro stairs.

It had been one week since last Friday when she was kissed and refused to enter the ladies' room cubicle with him. She took a seat at a small round table where she could view all directions. There was the luxuriant-in-summer Luxembourg, across the street. Too early today for the statues to be flirting with nightfall, or sex or love, and it was not summer, it was freezing. There was the manager in a black tuxedo, slicing *tarte tatin,* she could sniff the burned sugar across the room. There was a lone unshaven professor in the left corner who had not been kissed in twenty winters. Lips chalked, at the corners. She could not help him. There was a tourist in a red-striped button-down, waiting for the glamour of the City of Light to electrocute his life; he would die satisfied on the Left Bank. There was no boy with dimples who had made her dream of his flesh. She'd prayed for grace. She'd returned, holding her dignity like a breakable glass cup. Grace was finding fantasy disintegrated by a sudden hailstorm, disappeared in a destructive March wind. Maybe he'd been murdered. There was no one to ask, not the new waiter who was eyeing her pearl on its long chain, nested beside the miraculous medal that nested in her determined cleavage, lovely even for a woman past her prime.

And then there was one more message. Her portable bleeped. Outside, the storm had spent its strength, there were sudden sun rays piercing back into the gardens. The message read *Comment allez vous?* He used the formal address, "Vous." *I am in the park, come and meet me before I go to work? I am sorry I missed our rendezvous, I fell asleep.*

She entered the garden unhurriedly, past its signature green metal chairs, all empty. She nodded to her right, to those starkly ravished Medici lovers and their hovering Grecian-god-protector. Let her eyes scan the naked spaces, the bare branches and the storm-scattered clay gravel, and the new glare of late sun on the fountain below the stone stairs, there where small boys were not launching their tiny sail-boats with sticks, not today. And there he was. So he had not been murdered. He approached her as diffidently as a courtier at his first dance. Newly shaven, his face petal-smooth, a neck vein pulsed. He did not kiss her. He extended his hand. They shook hands. She made small talk. —How is your work? oh you have two jobs? are you origi-nally Parisian or from the country? so what do you do when you are not working?

—I see my pals, he fidgeted, looking at his watch. In fact I must meet one at the fountain of Saint Michel at five o'clock, it is a quarter 'til, now, I'll call you again and we might meet again for a longer time, is that acceptable? And he was gone.

—Paris is my only lover, she told Francesca, who was smiling like a sunrise at one more stranger. It was summer, now. Fully green. Fully floral. The war was not over. Times have never been worse, they agreed, unable to cry tonight.

CAGE

Around the corner from my fancy East Side school there's a window on Lexington Avenue with cages in it. At home I live in a cage too. It's green, wallpapered with floor-to-ceiling bookshelves and expensive paintings on our walls; my father collects them, he likes landscapes. They yell at the dinner table, making points with the sil-verware. They growl like starved animals at each other every night when he comes home from his office on Fifty-Seventh Street. He calls my mother a culture vulture. He never likes her friends. They yell at feeding time, especially. We're locked in our apartment and I have to listen to it. School is the getaway, snobby rich girls but they don't yell. The shop is the real escape. I see it on a Monday, I dream about it for two weeks before I ever go in. Silky animals. I love animals. But for two weeks I won't go in. Then I stop in front, it's the monkey. She's in the window in a cage, my silken savior.

The cage is gold metal about three-feet-high and square, thin slats and shiny. The lock gleams too, it looks like a yellow sapphire. She is squatting in it, butt to the sawdust, a piece of bark and lettuce and old carrots, that's all. How can she eat that? I hate vegetables, I like lamb chops and apricot juice. I decide right then I could bring her meat tomorrow. And a brownie. I promise her I will, through the window, through the cage, through our brains.

Her eyes are turned-earth with tiny blue veins around the pupils and a film over them like milk. She's scratching inside her ear and I think she's crying. She's as big as my mouse doll on my bed in my room, but the mouse is bigger than any real mouse. And the mouse has clothes. The monkey is all naked and clean bright white fur with tan tufts on her ribs and at her armpits. She shows her tiny teeth, a speck of lettuce stuck in front. The way she sits I can see her bright pink parts too. It's her tragic milk eyes that make me want to stay.

I go inside the shop and gag right away. It stinks inside. The guy in the grey cowboy hat grunts at me and lets me edge near the monkey in his window. Don't touch, little girl, ok? You can look but don't stick your fingers in there, she might bite you.

I say ok, really softly. I guess he doesn't hear. Did you hear? I say yes again, very softly.

The rank stink of about fifty different animal bodies makes me feel sick but I just want to get closer to the white monkey. I can't help seeing it all. I look quickly as if I had to memorize it all for a test and then I can get back to the pearl-eyed monkey and get out. But she is crying.

There's an open-topped tank, two feet long. It has a red sign that says Piranha. He's no real color, just darker than the water, and floating. He sees me. There's a wall of dogs whining in different octaves. All hungry. A wall of cats. I hate cats. They're the only animal I hate. A wall of birds, peach and green, turquoise, yellow, red, all cawing and pecking for love. I say, I'll be there in a minute, little birds. There are wooden shelves of litter and dog cereal and a skinny metal rack of seed branches losing some seeds to the floor, and a turn-around stand that has rubber mouse toys and bell toys and fake fur. The guy in the grey cowboy hat is sitting high in an iron swivel barbershop chair at his counter, with a *New York Times* all spread open across his lap. My father reads that paper too. I remember how I don't like barbershops; my father took me to one once, and they cut off all my curls.

So you like animals, little girl? He's being nice but I don't feel like talking to him. I want to talk to the white monkey. She's got her face against her gold bars, pressed so hard they are making little dents in it.

Hi, beautiful lady, I say. I know she's waiting for me. I want to pet her silky fur. I want to save her. I know she can't like the stink in here any more than I do. I'm staying and holding my breath just for her.

Get out of here, little girl. I turn around. The man has his face in his paper. It wasn't him that said that. Hurry up, darlin'. This is no good place for a child. I'm turning around and around because who's saying that? Please, sweetie, get your pretty little ass out of here.

It's the white monkey. Absolutely.

The man in the barbershop chair is not there anymore. He's up right next to me and he has his hands starting to move and tickling all over my body and then they're looking for my panties and they feel like cat claws and I'm kicking and the monkey is jumping jumping jumping in her cage. I can see her teeth while I'm fighting for my life.

I lose the fight. He has me against a shelf, so I cannot move at all, and he finds between my legs with all his fingers and he pushes them inside me and he won't stop and he won't stop and then he makes a noise louder than all the noise in there and pulls me back against him and then against the shelf he presses me with his pants rocking at me and then he grabs himself inside his pants and he stops looking at me, stops touching me, he's rubbing himself, harder, and harder, and harder and his head is back-tilted and twisting side to side and that's when I can crawl loose and away and he lets me, I think he just lets me and I'm gone and how can I tell anybody, I can't. She warned me and I didn't listen. I nightmare about her every night until I'm a woman. Grownups belong in cages. Most of them. I never go home the same way again. New York is a city where you can take a different street, a different back alley and a round-the-block sidewalk to get to the same place. That's what I do. I never even cross her window again. Her gold cage.

"The blackbird whistling / Or just after."

—Wallace Stevens

Beautiful Soon Enough

There is a white mist swathing the chapel like an infant and like a shroud and like a rip in the fabric of suspicious time, and a new fabric woven just for this night. And she approaches it. An odd little woman. Small. Not dwarfed, but tiny, dressed in long and used black velvet.

She's never seen it like this, like a phantom out of fairy tale and hope and dream and innocence. Out of holy hope and time and Jesus, it's too lovely. Fog, pale soft smoldering, covering the topmost thin spire and all the dome and all but the width of steps she mounts. Mounts, and the weighted door ahead that leads her to a circle of carved wooden saints, how did they know she was coming? Mounts, and she walks as if she lives in this house, familiar as a bell.

Choose me, choose me, choose one, pick a card, this one dear, here. The fog is tolling like a call for vespers, and she touches the pedestal, a slow caress with her short thumb. Good pilgrim, she places a tiny pebble there.

He's a statue different from the crucified, different from the infant, different from the loin-clothed dead man in a mother's arms.

He's maturity and care and upright and his hands open, his palms turn up at his robed sides. And the paint on his beautiful breast glows, chipped old paint, worn, but a glow.

Sacred heart fill my heart, sacred heart let this heart love, sacred heart teach my heart. She knows her prayers as though she invented them. She learns them all anew in the instant. He, of this shrouded night. He, of this lifetime. He. Dear God. She's in love with His Son again. She wants to join the monastery.

Odd little woman. Tiny. Dressed in long velvet that trails the floor, gathering dust, and a smile for ghosts, for medieval stones and doors, for the inlay and rosewood organ, huge, on its dais, which she immediately is longing to play.

But her fingers have always been too stubbed and too little to span the octaves, so she never became the concert pianist she'd ached to be. Never. And her legs were short and barely could reach the pedals of an organ. Still, she practiced. She has a possession, her stunning mother's upright piano, which she has crated and sent to wherever she moved, from town to town and country to country. To touch it as she walks by it. A mindless caress. To play it when none hear the notes she cannot reach.

Her mother is long dead and with the shadows. Disappointed that she was not a pretty child, not a pretty woman. Too short. Too stubbed. Too fervent. Too worried. Never wed. Yet, she had played until her hands cramped and she would have to bathe them in heated water and salts, work the pained joints with foreign olive oil.

She hummed cantatas and concertos and hymns of every denomination and waited to be chosen by fate, waited for good things to happen to her.

While her arms hung in a kind of daily surrender at her sides, this is my life, she thought, my life. One eye looked sideways, as though at ghosts, it always had.

Crossed, it saw the monks filing in for their final service of the day, fog clinging still to their stooped, caped shoulders, taking their places in a divided aisle before the quiet, and their cross. It saw the bald and lame one who climbed the dais to the precious organ and laid his healthy hands upon its silent keys, waiting for his moment. It saw the last light crouched in a corner, and the candle that flared brighter at it. She wanted to belong. Here.

The mother superior thought it a poor idea. The stranger was neither a Catholic nor a nun. The answer was no.

Still, she bought a narrow house in the town. With an entry that let her mother's piano in, and a stern sitting room and a steep stair to an attic with a single bed. On the cobble-stoned hill leading to the chapel. And she decided to spend the rest of her days overlooking this landscape made for somber penitents or angels, and the order that lived in silence there, but for organ music, an occasional lute like a misplaced love song, and sermons that broke into silence, meaning all the world to her. She came to every mass, every morning, noon and nightfall. Hunched velvet, in a corner, greying curls in a knot above her collar. Face buried into her own hands when she stood up to pray. No light, no thought should interfere.

A stark winter squirrel, she hummed with them when they sang and sang with the organ when it filled all space, her walleye on the lame brother who was allowed to play. Prayed every prayer and knelt to every homily and longed to take communion with them but she did not belong. The mother superior was clear about that.

Sainted God, Strong God, Eternal Saint, have pity on us. She bent forward and she touched the stone floor as they did, and straightened her small spine and touched her forehead and her breast from left to right as they did, and repeated the incanted words as they did. And she returned to her attic bed on the hill that led to the chapel and she transcribed words of the soft-browed brother who preached each sermon. From her memory, into a parchment-papered book. In him was a shining. And a severity she obeyed. And she translated his words into English which was her mother tongue, and she smiled at him three times a day, a blessing. A devotion. Her notebooks fattened. The mother superior looked through her, she did not really exist.

If the severe brother saw her, he nodded, gravely. She saw his heart. Skinned as an apple. It glowed.

She edged to the side of the chapel where the brothers knelt. To be further away from the mother who disapproved. To breathe. With them. On their side.

She bought an expensive red wine and drank it alone in the late slow evenings and hummed Pachelbel and hymns, and waited to be touched. By the carved statue. By the brother. His cloth. His cape. His tapered hands. By the statue. Its open palms. She wanted to play, for him. To make the chapel notice. To gift the chapel on the hill with her exploding soul. They all were busy. A daily routine. A small town. Polished statues. Replaced tapers. A religious order. Bells. Whispering. Ovens. Washing. Melted wax. Sweeping.

And she: lusted for the chapel organ. It filled her reveries, two flights up, doors on each landing, closed against night. It lured her and she pounded it, and trilled it, her head inches from a keyboard as she twisted the insufficient shape to reach and to reach its music, its keys. At dawn she descended her stairs and climbed the hill and returned at noon and returned at dusk. She inquired, only once, if she might play the instrument, just alone, when no one was there, not at mass, but when they were busy, when they were not there. She did play a piano, she asserted in nearly a whisper. She was told to wait, and then refused with little interest.

Still she came three times a day to mass. In between, she shopped for her morning bread, a bit of red meat to cook, and good Burgundy wine, and was greatly ignored. A stranger in a town that kept to itself mostly. They knew she was there. That was about all. She walked the somber landscape in all weathers, her long cape fraying at the hem, her mind as well. An interloper at the door of a silent monastic community whose job was to pray throughout the day. Yet, she waited for a beautiful thing to happen.

She heard every liturgy and wept only for the music. She envied the lame brother. The thin sister who played a lute once in a great while, when passages were read from the Song of Songs.

She hungered for the Eucharist, and finally they tolerated her in the communion line, eyes averted. She touched the pedestal of the mature and open-handed Christ on her way in and on her way out. She imagined embracing it. Climbing it. Pressing her bold heart to its glowing one, unashamedly. Inside the velvet folds, her nipples softened.

The brother whom she now loved, nodded, very occasionally. His transcribed words lived in her ravenous notebooks, in two languages. A thing he did not know.

They found the words when they found her.

It was an afternoon in early May. The yew tree bending lower, the plane trees were green again. Wisteria colored the vines that clung to the outside of her house. As ignored as she was, no one had seen her pass in many days. Or occupy that corner on the wrong side, behind the brothers. That odd little woman, the brother thought, randomly as a blackbird's flight. They had never spoken. And still.

He knew the narrow house. Had in fact noticed her unfocused eye. Her entering and exiting, some days. Her solitude, a sound he nodded to. That was all. But a small thing is a thing.

The next night, his dream troubled him. Vacant rooms and rooms and rooms and a single eye, hers, askance and following his step. And the next night, again the same. And rooms as though thieves had taken everything, everything in them, everything in every crack and every cupboard. And the small woman's terrible eye. After the third dream repeated, and after his morning mass and after his noon mass that day and before the daylight shifted its slant between a yew tree and its neighbors, he stood before her house.

They found her badly, on her second landing, her stub fingers rigid around the knob of that unopened door. She'd died on her own stair, never making it to Matins, Wednesday morning.

The transcribed pages were discovered later.

—A stranger came among us, he spoke, with tremendous strain in front of a very short pine box. She had no family, none present. When it was learned, one thin sister and the wine merchant came to bow their heads. —A stranger, the brother said again, a voice like wire. She came to our door and who among us loved her?

She was interred with nods and without further fuss, stark winter squirrel.

Undertow

Medieval Dubrovnik rises from the tide to the mountain, and its music hasn't been shattered yet. Years before the Serbo-Croat war-blood spits across its hills, yet again, those cobblestones blaze in the Adriatic sun. An ancient village built on slopes, it's like a smoked topaz in the coastal light.

A dictator's portraits hang next to crucifixes above wooden beds in every house, and up and down the stairs built into its hills, summer festivals bring music pilgrims to its altars. We're among them.

We're among them and there's a painter, Jacques, who wears a woolen black beret in the heat and travels with his plump and breathless wife, she plays the violin. She plays and he's memorizing new colors to use for the deaths of the sun. There are two cello soloists who play alone for the night heavens and need no audience. I hear them from our window. I never want to sleep. I use the soft pedal when I practice on the piano in the afternoon-dark salon, I don't want to be noticed yet. Not for that.

I have a knife-thin waist and I'm very young and on a summer holiday with my strict conductor-father and his elegant second wife. She wears thin white silk; she says it helps her to remain cool. I'm hot. I watch her, how she never stains. We meet the painter-violinist couple at a Friday concerto, and they invent a shared Sunday luncheon party on a monastery island, out there in the siren-songed Adriatic.

It'll take a motor launch to get there, an adventure. I've dreamed of sirens who waited for Odysseus: of luring. I want that word in my mouth. Luring. I want to sing like an ocean.

On Saturday, I'm riding in a crowd of black-eyed Croats, our bodies packed in like plumped fowl for the block. I'm a wild card. I want attention. On that crowded bus, I just allow my hip to rub against a full-lipped Serbian boy who's wearing pale cotton shorts, until we both know exactly what's happening, and we turn our heads away from one another so that no one notices. I blow him a daring kiss when my father and his wife and I leave the bus at our stop, and my father rages at me, because of the kiss.

On Sunday that same boy is the driver of our motor launch. I can't look at him.

The monastery lies some sea-miles out from the Dalmatian coast. I sit in the stern and stare at the water. The water's eyes are closed. The monastery is set in the middle of a glass-still lake. A tiny island inside an island, like a baby in a womb. I think how it's waiting to be born, how the nuns there will never know a man. We walk on boulders and over a wire-cabled bridge above a divide. We walk on dry air. We arrive at a public garden in the monastery grounds where our sumptuous luncheon is to be prepared. I'm learning to like elegance. I want to like white, and silk, like my father's wife. The painter Jacques, in his woolen black beret, his wife on his arm, my strict father and his pale wife and I are the monastery's guests. Jacques has influence.

I stare straight ahead. I walk faster than the rest. I'm eager as a hungry goat. I love how the boy blushes. I like his warning in careful English, when we land—this island gathers two different water currents, the side where we have beached is kind and receptive. The far side is dangerous, no one should enter the sea there or get the idea of swimming on that side—a word to the wise.

Everyone else smiles.

At that moment, Jacques and I have caught one another's glance and something is said in absolute silence, a sudden desire, stated. Desire is white in the center, and outlined in charcoal in places, and calculated in places, and modern, and metallic and obvious. We each want to see the dangerous side. Our party continues across the stones and the cabled bridge to our waiting meal. Course after course is served by young nuns in grey robes; I wonder why they're here, I wonder if they're very lonely. There's a peacock, crying on cue.

When our group is well fed and white-wine-dizzy, and lazy, and drowsy, and they're beginning to nap in the shade on mats—the painter and I catch each other's drift again. It's as if the others are being put into a deep sleep, in a magic mime play. With just a nod, we've agreed, and we follow one another away from the rest, headed for the tempting cliffs.

—Come.

I think for a minute of the Serbian boat-boy; but that'll wait. His mouth. This is equal, and exciting. The sea is wilier than any summer swimmer. We like this idea, no need to say so.

Come, the sea hisses. Come, test me.

The man and I climb back up and over the divide; across dry grasses and across the landscape to the opposite shore; and then on down to the sharp-faced drops. The cliffs, and rocks, and down a loose-dirt path, tossing off our sandals to better hold the ground with our bare feet. And soon we toss our clothing too and we jump naked from the high rocks. Diving, we hit a chilled silver embrace. The painter's palette has never brought such water to life. My muscles have never fought such a current. The undertow is alarming. Fighting. We're in love with the moment.

And it's instantly clear. The sea is shockingly rough. The rocks we've jumped from are jagged and sharp. The waves we're now in can smash us back against the cliffs at any moment, and we can be injured or killed. We laugh. We laugh out loud and shout out and make great sounds that are swallowed by the sea and its sounds. We hoot at the orchestra. We use up all our energy to swim in it, crazed with the pleasure of human and nature meeting in this combat. We thrash in it until we know we can't let ourselves become exhausted or how will we ever escape? No words again, we join our bodies with the power of the sea—and float, to let it help us, float, find a way back to any rock perch at all, loose, so it won't hurt, pause, to breathe and rest and cling to it, to let go and float or grasp or climb again before the next wave, and the next and the next and the next.

Full of the risk, and our successes, in some epiphany of his middle age and of my youth, we scale the cliff at last and we win. Naked, we find our abandoned shoes and clothes and cover ourselves. We're giggling hysterically. We've done something dangerous and forbidden and crazy and we're ecstatic. We return to the reawakening luncheon party, never admitting a thing. We've gone for a stroll.

On the way back in the motor launch, the boy with coal eyes tries and tries subtly for my attention. I'm indifferent. I'm grinning instead into the west wind, letting it rip at my hair with its fingers, and we're riding home on sunset's palette. I've made the painter happy.

•

I'm heading uptown.

It's a Sunday afternoon in New York City on upper Broadway. I'm wearing a white summer dress. Silk. People always say I've never lost my muscled body or my thin waist. My hair hangs long and loose. They look.

Broadway is rife with competing music. Competing skin. There's a kind of a game I play making eye contact with strangers. Forcing it. Forcing it when desire has no name. I don't remember when I began it. Maybe I always began it. Looking right at them until they have to meet my eyes and at least acknowledge me, at least look, maybe more, or turn away. It's like gambling. I do it all the time. In street crowds when I'm walking, in shops and lobbies and cafés and parks and subways, when I'm standing in a movie line, alone at restaurant tables: I play. When I win I feel alive. It doesn't matter who it is, young or old, or woman or man or baby. I like to make them know that I see them, force them to see me back. Just that. It matters.

There's a certain look coming toward me, heading downtown on the same street. I feel, rather than hear, a low-voiced cello's sound; a regret; no, a keening. A peacock's howl, not even its cry; no, stones, breaking.

His hands. Lovely huge hands. Paint, un-painted. Young blood cells. Summer, tearing. Soul fabric. I'm the one opening. As though naked; no; our skin removed; I have no skin. But I cannot seem to make any sound at all.

I've slowed to meet him head on. I can't play with this one. His linen jacket is all buttoned up to the neck in the hot sun. His head is thrust forward like an old turtle. But no, his shoulders are straightening, straightening and coming to bolder attention. His hands are lapis veins in a thin beige silk casing. The man coming toward me has eyes the color of a sea we fought.

We recognize one another. Jacques is a very elderly man now, walking so carefully, arm in arm as ever with his plumper wife. Our recognition comes with a leap in both our bodies. Never releasing his wife's arm, Jacques lifts his black hat with the other hand. The black beret tips at his touch like a Charlie Chaplin bowler. And he says to me —Remember Dubrovnik, and he walks on. No more. Broadway swallows us in its own Sunday.

IMPRINT

There is a story that is told in the Pacific nights, about the goddess of fire, when she was pursued by an overeager king. He was a
conqueror, and she didn't want to be conquered. She hid inside a
cave in the depths of her earth, red with tarnish, its walls of sculpted
flame points, silver-long and giant; at the end of a sixty-three mile
lava tube that skewed from the moon-scaped mounts of her island to
the cooler sea. And there, the one who was fire, made fire, made the

lava, was its river—left her imprint on the floor of her hardened flow. She crouched in her inner world, and she stooped there to plant love like a graffito: an imprint, ancient, raw, the flying vulva of the deity of all fires. She left her sign of womanhood, and nothing else there. She didn't want his chase, there. But she liked visitors.

•

The creature stretches and shows her breasts, nipples the shade of eggplants. She shakes a mantle of persimmon curls, her digits are fire-singed; one of her legs is also a hand, she uses it to stroke her own shape—as if to say, I like me. Don't you?

The visitor sees it almost immediately. Sprawled and iridescent on a jagged rock by the tide. And it winks at her, tongue licking at the sun, like a lizard.

The visitor settles, mimic-sprawls on an adjacent flat stone, at home in the presence of divinity. She doesn't stare. But she feels the fire, how its skin ripples like a single muscle.

The visitor is being observed, acknowledged by a nod, a trill in the water and in the wind around their two rocks. She lets her own thin fingers trail the ocean-sheen, gathers it like moving mercury, in her cupping hand.

The she-creature mimics her. Quick-shifts. Is the fire now, is more like a lizard, and still woman, too. White ash, for hair. Dazzling. There's a short branch in her lizard-hand, fashioned to help her to rise gracefully. She lifts it.

—So so so. Tell me who you are.

The visitor has come to an island to become honest.

—I don't know.

—So that's good. That's good. So so so. What do you have to eat? She's looking at the meager picnic dregs, an emptied water bottle.

The visitor knows she has nothing left to offer. And the lizard has vanished.

•

And it appears and disappears, everywhere, unannounced. There are no more questions, and it's early for replies. Sometimes, the "she" only stands there, stroking. A temptress. Sometimes, she is old. Sometimes, as though she might actually touch the observer with a dark and slow hand, singed fingers—she doesn't. With a camou-flaged hand that has trailed through the vines, and matches them—sometimes, she is a promise, and a possible friend.

The island lives in its own passionate spectacle. Volcanic. It thrives and cracks, and preens, and shimmies, spills, and rains in flame. De-stroys, and goes back to sleep.

The visitor is never unaware of it. How it is watching her. Wait-ing for her. She stays longer and longer on an island she's beginning to worship. She loves its black stones, those tiny, godly faces she finds in them. Loves the rain that tastes of fungus and salt and smoke. Loves the unseen, and its whispers. She stands like a lone heron on promontories of cooled lava, winds at her scalp. She begins to leave invented offerings: a meal, gathered; a garland of weeds; a dead red-fish, cleaned. She loves the nights, their frightening number of stars. On nights with no moon, she finds beaches where she wants to bathe alone and naked in the late hours just before total darkness; only a small distance from shark beds in the deeper water. In daylight, she finds rainforests where water drums the leaves, where she likes to rest beside rolled ferns, their uncoiling center stems, like slender pe-nises. They make her smile. She's sleepwalking; and sometimes she's awake.

She settles in to a place where she can smell the new earth form-ing. She likes to sleep on the ground, she thinks that it breathes. At night there are a thousand crickets, and the mallet-headed small brown owls circle, mindfully.

And, she has men, the way a wanderer in a garden tastes fruits.

She enjoys their differences, their thighs, their mouths; she has no plans for her life.

When she becomes pregnant it's neither important nor unimportant, it's a fact. She sits in her garden alone, watching things grow, her hand stroking her belly in circles. She hums to it. In the winter, she will give birth all alone, clinging to a smooth branch, hanging from it until her baby crowns between her lips, under a late sun.

She is full-voiced; screaming; and then silent as a death; and then, again, she is humming. She gives it her swollen breast. She treats the baby and herself like needy animals. Cleaning. Warming. Cooling. Feeding. Cleaning. Napping.

One green afternoon, she knows there is a thing she should do before the sun falls. She walks to the mountain, and there she carries her newborn to a high and open womb, to the crater's rim. The crater is where the one like a lizard—the woman who is fire—lives.

A flock of long-tailed white swallows falls into the fog. A single twist of platinum rises, a greeting. The mother holds up her girl-child. —Look, she whispers.

There's a light drizzle that alters the ambient tint from sulfur and old burn, to a low shining. The clouds are massing, and a shadow is darkly in the center of a sudden, round, full-spectrumed bow. Circle no more huge than her dead grandmother's vanity mirror, loose in the volcano's crater, and seen, and unseen, and seen.

How it stays. How its arms are raising in a dreadful benediction, unless what she is seeing in that center is the self, such a shadow.

She sings out in a language she has never spoken before —*E ola mau, e Pele e! Eli'eli kau mai!* Long life to you, Pele.

And then again, her whisper, holding up her girl, to be seen. —Look!

Pleased, the one whose body fills the crater bowl, red sand, and stone, and fire-mantled, bright-tongued, chanting—a woman, and smoke, and familiar—reaches for her visitor. —Yes, you're mine, she says. That's what you came here to know.

The woman and child are licked in flames; long, and slowly.

Once again. —Tell me who you are.

—A visitor.

—Do you want to stay?

•

There is love, and there is not. There are leaves, and there are not. But there is/was/ever...fire, and some god, some start, and shape, like a changed autumnal blood...black imprint of a garden, of an endlessly mended woman, soon enough.

•

Drunken with her joy of it, she dances slowly and low to the ground, and then faster to a drum only she hears, and faster still, around the crater's lip. There, where lava is solid and cool, there where it is cracked and teasing steam, there where it is innocent, there, where it receives her fall.

There is a story that is told of a woman pursued by fire. Consumed. Of her child, who survived.

Contract

The contract they made when it began had this for content: When or if we do not love as we do now—we can stop the engine. That's it. We've said it. All I have is you. And they signed it, their fingertips dipped first in a hundred-dollar bottle of red wine and then in each one's perfume. The ink they used to sign the page stained their hands like henna tattoos. They did not wash for a week.

The white and shiny car was found. The husband who outlived her did as they'd promised. Tasted her ashes before he gave the wind its portion. The problem was that he did not die quickly afterwards, as predicted, that predictions are unreliable, that there were a thousand more places to make love. More. That he lived, and continued to count. A man with eyelashes longer than hers.

It began with the husband. —Let's not have children, love. Let's be only "us." Like this. Forever. Like this, was traveling. Like this, was fingers and tongues and thirst and thrusting and riding, in a hundred places in a year; they would count. Between the Bombay garden shadows. Past-midnight low light, in a town square in Tuscany. He laughed, —Right here in front of God and everyone? —Yes, she said, leading. A rooftop in the East Village under fireworks and then, sleet. In the Plaza Hotel elevator, one hand on the red Stop button, one demanding to be inside her, quickly. At the Montauk tide line, a stiffened winter deer washed up on the same sand. In a Denver road stop. In a hotel flame. With no curtains. With hunger. With steak. In a train station at dawn in Iowa. On the lake raft fronting a house they never owned.

They wanted to have made love in a thousand places before they died. They were dying; nothing to cry about, so was everybody.

The wife stopped it. My heart can burst now, she wrote on the hotel mirror in Barcelona, using nail polish the same color as the fuchsia orchids on their breakfast table. Then she drove the white shiny car until it burst. Nothing in their contract said that.

Scissors, Paper, Rock

It swerved through the room, striking a narrow slit into an opening that blinded him in one eye. The sister had thrown her scissors at the little boy. No one could forgive her. Just because he had been screaming for them.

Her life after that had no rewards. Ever. No one could love a child who had blinded her small brother. The word accident was eventually eliminated. She was a limb, cut. They could not look at her. And the little boy was sainted. Worshipped for his pain.

It was when they were both grown that the sister came to him, begging. And he said maybe. Come back in a week.

While he meditated on what he would do, the brother performed one of his many small and obsessive activities. Seated calmly at his hand-carved mahogany desk, he prepared a stack of blank sheets and carefully he folded each, in the right way. He lit the lamp with a high intensity bulb, focused. Then he removed a fine and sharp and silver scissors from the top left drawer and set to work: like strings of paper dolls, he produced the linked shapes, orbs, linked one to one. And then the colored pencils, these he used to draw and color in each eye, with a perfectionist's detail. And when he had finished his project, he placed and hung the strings of cutouts in garlands around his office. Still, he had not decided on an answer. She'd return in a week. By then he would know what to say.

He locked his office door and did not reopen it until the appointed morning.

He was an orderly man. A well-dressed man. A wealthy man. His good eye was the color of a dragonfly's wing, iridescent. His glass eye, carefully washed, carefully replaced every night with an attendant and very quiet curse, was in fact a pretty object. Not very different from the king-sized marbles which he had won and collected for many years. One such marble was something he always carried in a pocket. Not vaunting it. But because.

It was ten o'clock. A summer morning. It was raining. And his sister was at his door. He let her in, saw her shudder as she observed his macabre or playful handiwork, which was it—strung from all angles. He allowed her to stand for a long time, and she did not take any liberty toward his room. She waited, as she had since they were angry siblings. And after—cut by the ones whose bloodlines she shared. She wanted to be forgiven.

This morning, she was not. She saw that now. Blackening, her plea was going to be refused. And then, the boy who would not give her what she needed, gave her his prized object. White and cool and round and perfect, from his pocket to her hand.

He waited until she had closed her fingers around it and held it silently. Waited until she cried for the first time in thirty years.

Then, one by one, he took down his paper cut-out decorations and carefully he folded them and these he gave to her as well. She had not moved.

No words between them. Ever. Or any who could speak for them.

Severed, she walked in the rain. Hindsight and its pruned branch, and the white perfect marble in her chapped hand.

NOTES

- The epigraph, "Moi, je mords la terre comme un fruit"…Me, I bite the earth like a fruit…is a line from an old and popular French song recorded by film star Jeanne Moreau.

- Philomel: L Philomela, fr. Gk Philomele, an Athenian princess who was raped by her brother-in-law King Tereus, en route to her own marriage, and, after having had her tongue cut out by him, she was later avenged and transformed into a nightingale. The nightingale in pastoral verse is symbolic of romantic love.

- Animalia: The Animal Kingdom.

- "White Wings They Never Grow Weary" is from Carolyn Forché's book *Gathering The Tribes*.

- Pele is the goddess of all that is fire in the mythos of the Pacific.

- "Fling the emptiness out of your arms / into the spaces we breathe" is from Rainer Maria Rilke's "First Duino Elegy" (translated by Pierre Joris).

- Black and white photos/photo-montages and cover art for *Beautiful Soon Enough* are the author's.

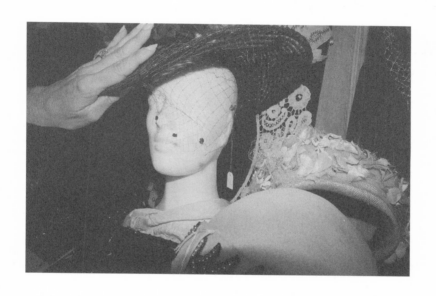

Acknowledgments

I am grateful to the editors of the following publications in which stories from this book have appeared (some in earlier versions): *Agni*, "Pas De Deux À Trois," "A Friday Desdemona," "Troika for Lovers"; *Confrontation*, "Donkeys"; *Nimrod International*, "Contract"; *Poetry International*, "Philomel"; *Van Gogh's Ear*, "For Flame And Irresistible"; *Fairy Tale Review*, "Window."

My immense gratitude to Cyrus Cassells and to Robin Lim, for the kind years of reading over my shoulder, and the faith that it would happen. And to Theodore Sturgeon, with memory and care, for the poetry of story, and for once teaching me the meaning of "Tandy."

ABOUT THE AUTHOR

Margo Berdeshevsky currently lives in Paris. Her poetry collection, *But A Passage In Wilderness*, was published by Sheep Meadow Press in December 2007. Her honors include five Pushcart Prize nominations and special mention citations in the 2008 & 2009 Pushcart Anthologies, the Robert H. Winner Award from the Poetry Society of America (ms. selected by Marie Ponsot), the *Chelsea* Poetry Award, *Kalliope*'s Sue Saniel Elkind Award (ms. selected by Laura Mullen), honorable mention in the Pablo Neruda Award selected by BH Fairchild, a place in the Ann Stanford Awards (selected by Yusef Komunyakaa), & Border's Books/ *Honolulu Magazine* Grand Prize for Fiction. Her works have been published in leading literary journals including *Agni*, *The Southern Review*, *The Kenyon Review*, *Pleiades*, *New Letters*, *Poetry International*, *Runes*, *Pool*, *Margie*,

Nimrod International, Europe, Siècle 21, Frank, Indiana Review, Another Chicago Magazine, The Southern California Anthology, Many Mountains Moving, and *Van Gogh's Ear.* Recent exhibitions of her photographs, montages & "visual poems" have been at The Pacific Center of Photography in Hawaii, La Galerie Etienne De Causans, La Librairie Galerie Racine in Paris. Her interview & translations of French hip-hop star MC Solaar appeared in *Rattapallax.* Her Cuban photos illustrate the book *Cuba Satisima,* from Descartes & Cie, in France. *Vagrant,* a poetic novel, is next at the gate. She wrote her *Tsunami Notebook* following a journey to Sumatra in Spring 2005, to work in a survivors' clinic in Aceh. Her visual poem series *Les Ombres de Versailles* was seen at the Parisian Gallery Benchaieb. She was born in New York City, where she had a first career as an actress, performing in the world premieres of Harold Pinter's *The Basement* & *The Tea Party,* David Hare's *Slag,* worked in the companies of Lincoln Center and Joseph Papp's Public Theatre, toured the USA as Ophelia, and was nominated for a television Emmy award, for a country western drama in which she had her head in an oven, but was saved by a neighbor who prayed for her.